DONE
WRONG

Also by Eleanor Taylor Bland

Gone Quiet
Slow Burn
Dead Time

D O N E
WRONG

E L E A N O R
T A Y L O R
B L A N D

ST. MARTIN'S PRESS .... NEW YORK

LIBRARY OF CONGRESS CATALOGING-IN-PUBLICATION DATA
Bland, Eleanor Taylor.
    Done wrong: a Marti MacAlister mystery / Eleanor Taylor Bland.
       p.   cm.
    ISBN 0-312-13053-8
    1. MacAlister, Marti (Fictitious character)—Fiction. 2. Afro-American police—Illinois—Chicago—Fiction.
    3. Policewomen—Illinois—Chicago—Fiction.   4. Chicago (Ill.)—Fiction.
I. Title.
PS3552.L36534D65   1995
813'.54—dc20   95–9974
                                                                                   CIP

First Edition: July 1995

10 9 8 7 6 5 4 3 2 1

This is dedicated with great affection and appreciation to my agent, Ted Chichak.

Special thanks to very special ladies, my editor, Anne Savarese, and my publicist, Karen McDermott.

To my sons, Kevin and Todd, for their very practical and necessary support.

To my grandsons, Anthony and Todd Jr., who help me keep my life in perspective.

To four uniquely supportive women whom I greatly admire: Sara, Barbara, Susan, and Nancy.

For technical assistance, thanks to Dave Bockrath; Michael Bowen; Tom Borla; Phyllis Dex; Michael Dymmoch; Eunice Fikso; Margaret "Marge" Freund; Aaron Hainesworth, Boy Scouts of America; Lt. Hugh Holton, CPD; Ida Blanchard-Jones; Duane Mathis; Virginia MacDonald, super fan; Thomas Nickel, R.N.; Jerome Pierzak, Ph.D.; Andy Podraza; Reginald Spencer, Lake County Museum Services; Dennis Smiter; Ron Straff, R & R Gun Shop; Investigator John Sherwood, Waukegan Fire Department; Officer Edna White, CPD; John Rorabech and John Hamlin, Lake County Coroner's Office.

DONE
WRONG

By the time Julian Cantor climbed the five flights of stairs to the roof of the parking garage, he was gasping for breath. It had been months since he'd worked out. Maybe, after tonight, he would start again. The enclosed stairwell was cold, but out of the wind, at least. Julian leaned against the door for a minute, inhaling deeply. He turned up his collar and pulled his knit cap as far below his ears as it would go. Then, hunching his shoulders, he stepped outside.

The wind whipped the door shut behind him. Icy gusts of sleet stung his face. Winter had come early this year, and it was late February. It seemed as if the days would come slate grey and dismal like this forever. His military-issue parka would keep him warm in subzero weather, but a chill caused more by weariness than by weather had seeped into his bones. He felt as if he had been cold forever, a coldness that sun or summer warmth would never dissipate.

Julian shoved his gloved hands into his pockets and moved to the corner of the roof, partially shielded by the stairwell. Snow had been plowed into dirty mounds. Despite the darkness and the isolation and height from the street, he felt exposed and turned to see if anyone was standing behind him. His spine prickled. He was alone. No wire. His partner was a level below and out of earshot. His weapon was so cleverly concealed that he felt unarmed.

The lit stairwell was empty. Looking over the ledge, he saw that the sidewalk below was deserted. Across the street, the hospital was a contrast of light and darkness and shadow. On its roof, a helicopter sat ready to respond to another emergency. He turned again, felt the snow-covered concrete ledge hard against the small of his back. Facing Cottage Grove Avenue, he identified shapes and forms that seemed flat against the cloud-filled sky. A smoke-stack—the power plant. A single spire—not a church, just part of one of the Park District's buildings. The Roundhouse, built for the 1893 World's Fair. The Inter-Library Loan Building. Idly, he wondered how many people the brick and mortar had outlasted.

The wind picked up, slapping at his face. Its whistle muffled the sound of a distant siren until the ambulance came closer, its scream sharp now, then abruptly silent.

Where were they? Had they been here and left? He had planned to be on time, but some reluctance held him back. Not the cold. He had been on the street all winter. He was grateful to be cold and dry. Cold and wet was a bitch. So was waiting.

He had lingered in a doorway for a few minutes on his way here, sipping coffee, not caring as it burned his lips or his tongue. Not caring. The street did that. All of this would soon be something he might have imagined, or dreamed. What made this real—his thinking that it was so? He didn't care. Not tonight. It was too cold.

Below, closer to the corner, a door slammed. Someone was taking the elevator. Julian moved farther away from the lit stairwell, knowing that even in the darkness he would be seen. He kicked at a pile of snow with the tips of his boots. Long minutes passed before the elevator reached the top of the shaft. In the skewed rectangle of light, two men emerged, one short and thin and the other tall and fat enough to waddle.

They came toward him, bending forward in the wind, coats flapping. When they got close enough he could see the glowing tips of cigarettes, and even though he'd stopped smoking months ago, he longed for just one quick drag.

The men walked to the ledge and looked over. Julian stood beside the shorter of the two, and without speaking, they exchanged packages. The one Julian took was heavier than the one he gave them.

He waited for them to leave. Instead, the shorter man said, "Hey

'Nam Man, what's this we hear you're asking about some cop, Johnny MacAlister?"

Bile rushed to his throat. "I wasn't asking," he said. "I was repeating."

"Repeating what?" the short man asked, gouging out a handful of snow from the dirt encrusted pile. "The boss wants to know."

"Somebody dropped MacAlister's name three, four nights ago."

"Oh?" The man cupped one hand, crushing the snow into a lumpy ball.

"Yeah. Just some guy. I don't know who he was. I thought maybe Estlow would want to know."

Shielding a lighter, the taller man lit another cigarette. Smiling, he handed it to Julian.

Julian inhaled deeply. They couldn't see that his hand was shaking. His gloves were too thick. He inhaled again.

"Why was this guy talking about MacAlister?" the short man asked, weighing the snowball in his hand.

"I didn't hear nothing but the end of the conversation. That was what I was trying to find out."

How in the hell could it have gotten back to them? He hadn't said anything to anyone except Murphy and Jamison. He inhaled again. How much did they know?

"Here, let me light you another," the short one offered.

Before Julian could reply, the tall one seized his arm and twisted it behind his back until Julian thought he could grab his own neck. The pain was so intense that he gasped, but was unable to scream.

"Have another cigarette, Cantor."

They knew who he was. Before he could speak, they crammed something wet into his mouth, pushed it up his nostrils. Snow. Damned snow. He couldn't speak. The cold exploded inside his head as he tried to breathe. He struggled as they lifted him over the edge, and tried to spit out the snow that filled his mouth as the snow-covered sidewalk rushed up to him.

Across the street, from a third-floor room, a woman watched from her hospital bed as an angel flew past her window. "Thank you, Jesus," she murmured, smiling. Then, drowsy from the drugs dripping into her vein, she slept.

1

Marti MacAlister woke up all at once. What had awakened her? Outside, tires whined as a car tried to get out of the ice and snow. She must have pulled the sound into her dreams, where it became the drone of a small airplane plummeting to the ground. But was that what woke her up? She heard a thump. A tree branch? Uneasy, she reached for her gun.

She went to the door, listened, then opened it. As she eased into the hallway, Bigfoot, her family's Heinz fifty-seven, about the size of a Saint Bernard, came to Theo's door. Did Bigfoot hear something, too? Marti made a quick tour of the house. When she was satisfied that it was the car that had awakened her and not an intruder, she returned to her room.

She put the gun away and tried to relax against the pillows. Fragments of her dream began to nag. A skyscraper, a hot air balloon, a gigantic bird. Julian Cantor. He had died Sunday night or early Monday morning, when he fell from the roof of a parking garage. Because he was Jewish, the funeral would be held as soon as possible. It was Wednesday now. She should have called his wife. She felt guilty. After all, Rachel Cantor had come to her house the morning after Johnny's death. Not that Marti remembered seeing her, but one of the wives had kept track of visitors with a guest book. Rachel wouldn't remember much about today either. It might never occur to Rachel that Marti hadn't come, or that she should have.

Julian and Johnny hadn't worked under the same lieutenant, but they were both narcs. And they both died accidentally. How easy was it for someone to accidentally slip over a ledge that was at least four and a half feet high? Were they being kind to Rachel, as they had been kind to her, officially calling Julian's death an accident while privately insisting it was suicide? Would Rachel ever know what really happened on that roof? Would Marti ever know what happened to Johnny in that beat-up Chevy parked in a cemetery almost three years ago?

"No," she had told her captain. "No. Johnny isn't dead. His watch is over in two hours. He'll be back. We didn't say good-bye."

That morning she had awakened with him warm beside her, touched the sweat that glistened along his spine as she adjusted the blanket he'd pushed off. She had kissed his face, nuzzling a shadow of beard that was scratchy against her cheek, smelled the Dial soap he always used to scrub off his street persona. He stirred, said "Ummmm," breathed deeply again. If she had known, she would have awakened him.

His partner had ID'd him. She couldn't look at what a .38 caliber bullet shot at close range had done. She could remember how the dark angles of his face—high cheekbones, cleft chin, widow's peak, deep-set eyes, and prominent brows—seemed to soften when he looked at her. When she was alone, with the lights out and the house quiet, she could almost hear his voice, husky with passion as he whispered her name. She could almost feel his fingertips tracing patterns on her thighs.

The day after Johnny's funeral she had cooked all of his favorite foods. Ham hocks and mustard greens, red beans and rice, pigs' feet in port wine, fried buffalo and catfish, a smoked ham scored with cloves, corn bread, key lime pie. She set the table and refused to let anyone near it until he came home. At eleven o'clock that night, long after the children had gone to bed and everyone else had gone home, she wrapped everything and put it in the freezer. Then, for the first and only time, she cried.

One day she packed the photo albums away instead of going through them and reliving the past. That same night she stopped sitting alone in the living room after the children were asleep, listening to the tapes Johnny had sent while he was in Vietnam. Johnny, who was always so quiet, was with her on that sofa, telling her what it was like growing up with his mother, who was alcoholic, and his father, strict and silent and quick to give whippings, and how he missed and worried about his sister, who had left home young and not kept in touch. Unable to part with his Vietnam tapes and afraid that continuing to listen to them would become some kind of madness, Marti mailed them to her brother in Colorado.

Next, she put Johnny's collection of fifties and sixties records in storage. Johnny had loved to dance. Sometimes, when they were both working second watch, they'd come home after midnight, tired and hungry. Johnny would play their songs, and they would slow-dance while supper warmed.

Two months later, she walked away from the house they had shared for ten years. There, she couldn't sleep through the night because she kept hearing phantom sounds—Johnny's key in the lock, his footsteps on the stairs. His robe hung on the bathroom door, and she would lean against it and stroke it every morning, inhaling his cologne. Momma said she had to let go.

Now, advertisers had discovered their music. That commercial had been on TV when she came home tonight. She didn't know what the product was and the words had been changed, but every time she heard the melody she saw Lake Michigan in the moonlight and felt the sand, gritty and cool against her shoulders, and remembered Johnny's breath warm on her neck.

Momma was right, you didn't get over it, you got used to it. *What if* and *if only* became *never*. It got better when she moved to Lincoln Prairie, came to live with Sharon and her daughter, Lisa. Marti and Sharon had been best friends since grade school. Marti shared the pain of Sharon's divorce, Sharon shared Marti's grief when Johnny died. Now they shared expenses and child rearing and told each other most of their secrets.

Sometimes there were nights like this, when she did her job, arrested the right perp, got home too late to see her kids, went to sleep in her single bed and woke up before daybreak, depressed and alone. It still hurt, but not like it used to. She didn't ever want to hurt like that again.

Outside, the wind blew strong and violent. Another tree branch snapped under the weight of the ice and thudded on the roof. She went to the window. Everything was etched in ice—trees, bushes, wires. The snow had a shiny glaze. It was beautiful to look at, but treacherous when you had to be outside. Subzero temperatures had kept schools closed for two days.

Marti and her partner, Vik, had gone out to question a suspect tonight. The guy ran out the back door. They chased him for three blocks, slipping and sliding through unplowed alleys before cornering him in a garage. He fired one shot. It took half an hour to talk him into surrendering his weapon and coming out. Their teeth were chattering as they hustled him into a squad car. Marti's fingers and toes and ears hurt from the cold.

She was so wired when she got back to the precinct that after the perp confessed, she wrote out her notes and typed all of her reports despite her physical exhaustion. Thinking about it now, the adrenaline started pumping again. The thrill of pursuit, Johnny said. Something like this was a daily routine in Chicago. It seldom happened in Lincoln Prairie, and was one of the few things she missed about the city.

Unable to sleep, she went downstairs to the kitchen and turned on the light over the sink. The room became warm and cozy. When she first came here she had avoided this room, but now the yellow walls and the Boston ferns that hung from the long, narrow windows cheered her. Marti made a cup of herb tea, hoping she was selecting one that would make her drowsy.

Sharon came in while the tea was steeping. "Wind," she said, rubbing her eyes. Barefoot, she was just over five feet tall. Her purple and turquoise caftan moved in graceful folds as she sat down at the table.

"Tea?" Marti asked.

"No. I don't want anything that will make me think I might want to keep my eyes open." The multicolored beads that bound the dozens of braids in Sharon's weave clicked as she put her arms on the table and her head on her arms. She closed her eyes. "Wind," she said again. "And ice. Every time a branch hits the roof I wake up. I hope the power lines don't come down. Do we get faster repair service because you're a cop?"

"Have you noticed the trucks salting or plowing the street any sooner since I moved in?"

"Oh well, we can't have it all. I should have bought that house on the block where our alderman lives. At least I don't have to worry about burglars. Did you just get home? I thought I heard you come in a couple of hours ago. What time is it? No, don't tell me. Come eight-thirty, my students will be ready for me. I want to pretend I got enough sleep so I can make believe I'm ready for them."

"What time did you get to sleep?" Marti asked. Sharon had been having trouble sleeping for several weeks now. Her ex-husband, who had remarried soon after their divorce, was expecting a baby with his new wife any time now.

"Why are you up at this hour?"

"That's not answering my question. Why don't you get something from the doctor to help you sleep?" Sharon didn't like taking medicine of any kind.

"I'm getting enough sleep."

"At least try to take a nap in the afternoon."

"Okay. Now, why can't you sleep?"

"A cop I knew died."

"Oh." Sharon opened her eyes. "I guess I will have some tea."

"I'll make it. You just keep sitting there with your eyes closed."

When Marti set two mugs on the table, Sharon sat up. "So, how did this cop die?"

"He fell off a roof."

"How did that happen?"

"Nobody seems to know."

"Was he a narc?"

Marti nodded.

Sharon spooned sugar into her mug, sipped the tea, made a face and added more sugar. "Nothing helps this stuff. It tastes like boiled weeds."

"It probably is," Marti said.

"How well did you know this cop?"

"Cantor. Julian Cantor. I didn't really know him at all. Johnny did."

"So you can't sleep because some cop you hardly knew fell off a roof? It's February twenty-second, Marti. Johnny died April third. You and Theo and Joanna always start getting depressed right about this time and stay that way until mid-April."

Sharon was right. Joanna's basketball game was off, Theo's grades were down, she was trying not to be cranky, and worse, they were approaching one of those occasions when having a father around was almost a requirement.

"Theo is going into Webelos this year, between Cub Scouts and Boy Scouts. You know how it is with Scouting—the dads get real involved. I haven't asked anyone yet, but I'm sure dads are supposed to take part in the ceremony. Most of the time Theo and Johnny spent together those last months had something to do with Scouting."

"Then that's why he's so quiet. It's worse than last year, Marti. I think you should talk to Theo's teacher. This guy is Mister Macho. Lambert's five six and balding, lifts weights, jogs, and eats yogurt and raw spinach for lunch every day. I don't think he likes me. I eat junk food and you know how I feel about exercise. Lambert's got this weird notion that boys should be tough. He actually suggested that I make another kid learn to write left-handed when he broke his arm last semester. He hasn't said three words to me since." Sharon shook her head. "Jed Lambert is not going to appreciate me telling him that Theo's the silent, sensitive type. But you could make an impression. Talk like a cop and give him a glimpse of your gun."

Sharon folded her arms, hugging herself. "Guns. God, I hate them." Beads clicked as she shook her head. "I'm amazed at how the three of you deal with your job, especially with what happened to Johnny. I don't know how you get up every day, put on your gun and go to work."

A branch scraped against the window as it fell to the ground.

"I'm not a worrier," Sharon said. "And you make working homicide seem almost like a normal six-A.M.-to-midnight job, but it isn't, and I hate being reminded."

Sharon squeezed Marti's hand.

"And I know you. I know that you have to get up in the morning and put on that gun. Just like Julian Cantor. Just like Johnny. And you're so damned good at making it seem like an ordinary job, most of the time I forget to be afraid for you. I'm sorry to lay this on you, but sometimes I'm scared, even if you're not."

Marti's tea was cold. She thought about running down that alley, cornering that guy, talking him out. "Fear is good," she said. "It makes everything around you brighter, louder, clearer. Keeps you focused. Keeps you alert." She traced small circles on the table with her finger. "A lot of policing is routine. I don't do domestic calls. I don't make traffic stops. I don't serve warrants very often. I'm not a narc, so I don't go through doors. That's the dangerous stuff. Most of the time I get there after the action is over and I just look at dead bodies and crime scenes and talk with people. There's always the unexpected, but this is a pretty low risk job, as policing goes. When there is danger, stuff like you see on those real cop shows, then the rush is fantastic. Mentally and physically, I'm flying, I'm really high."

"That's how people describe being on drugs."

"Action is the average cop's drug of choice," Marti said. "My drug of choice. Johnny's. Julian Cantor's."

"What are you telling me?"

Marti looked out the window and beyond the light, into the darkness. She thought of Julian, in the dark, falling. She thought of Johnny, in the dark . . . There were so many things she knew about the job that she didn't want to think about, so much that she had never told Sharon. "I might get that rush a couple of times a year," she said. "Narcs get it almost every day."

Sharon thought for a few minutes. "Is that why you didn't fight it when they said suicide? Do you think Johnny wanted the high, that he died because he got reckless . . . or careless, going after a narc's fix?"

"Yes." It was a relief to say it aloud.

"Johnny wouldn't do that," Sharon said.

"You haven't experienced the high."

11

"You've been thinking this way ever since he died?"

"It is a kind of suicide, Sharon, not like what they said, but . . . kind of like Russian roulette."

"No," Sharon said. "Not Johnny."

"But I don't know that. As well as I thought I knew Johnny, I don't know that. And maybe I never will."

Marti listened to the wind and felt chilled.

2

As Vice Deputy Chief Joe Riordan walked out of the mausoleum, he was careful to stay well behind Rachel Cantor. Twice during the service, which was brief, she had turned to look at him. Her hostility was obvious. Displaced anger. As commander of the Narcotics Division he had been her husband's boss, but he was not involved in the day-to-day operations of a narc unit. Even so, Julian Cantor's dive off a parking garage roof while on duty would do nothing to advance his own career.

One of Riordan's Raiders had gone down. This was the first service-connected death in his department since he had taken command three years ago. His lieutenants competed to have the best arrest record. And now one of his men had gone down.

An icy wind whipped around the corner of the building, ruffling his hair as he lagged behind the mourners. He could see Cantor's lieutenant, Frank Murphy, who stood at least half a head taller than the rest of the contingent from the department. The wind and the sudden glare of sun and snow made Riordan's eyes water. His ears were so cold they hurt. He never wore a hat unless he was in uniform. Rachel had requested a low departmental profile, and he had been happy to comply. There were no reporters, no photographers. There had been the discreet whisper that Cantor might have been paying a late-night visit to a female "friend" after completing his watch, and the observation that Cantor's father, also a cop, had dropped dead of a heart attack at forty-nine. There was no mention of Cantor's undercover assignment. Nothing was said that would cause a reporter to pay more than the most cursory attention to his death.

Yesterday, Rachel had scoffed when Riordan told her the department had no idea why her husband was at a deserted hospital garage after midnight. He had suggested weariness, weather conditions, ice, to explain Cantor's fall from the ledge. When that didn't work he had asked how things were between them, if there were any problems, if Cantor seemed burned out or depressed. The little princess had bristled at the implications. "What are you covering up now?" she said angrily.

The "now" worried him. Did Cantor bring the job home?

"There's not even a mention in the newspapers," she said.

"They'll run the obit in the morning," he responded. He wanted to add that he had kept things quiet for her sake as much as anyone else's. "Julian was a good cop. He came from a long tradition of good Chicago cops," he said, trying to remind her of the conduct expected of her. Rachel had responded to that, biting back whatever else she wanted to say. He patted her shoulder, promised her all the resources the department made available to widows. He thought that was the end of it. But now she seemed angry again.

Snow crunched underfoot as Riordan walked to his car. His driver got out and opened the door. The engine was running, and Riordan welcomed the warmth. He removed his gloves and rubbed his hands together. He had told Frank Murphy to be at his office at eleven o'clock. It was almost eleven now. Leaning forward, he told his driver where to stop for lunch.

When Riordan got to police headquarters at 11th and State a little after one o'clock, Murphy was in the reception area. Despite the No Smoking sign, he was tipping ashes into a coffee cup and a thin layer of smoke floated above his head. Riordan's secretary, an older woman who, for political reasons, came with the job, gave Murphy a look of disgust. When she looked at Riordan her expression implied that this had better not happen again. Riordan was certain that the only reason she hadn't told Murphy to smoke someplace else was Murphy's connections.

Riordan noted that Murphy had gained a few pounds over the holidays. Probably all of that pasta he was eating now that he had married Sergeant Gianelli's girl. Murphy was tall enough to carry the extra weight, but his belt was buckled below his belly and he was beginning to look like a slob. As Murphy stood, taller than Riordan by almost a foot, Riordan wondered who would believe that this guy was an all-city basketball player eleven years ago.

Riordan motioned Murphy into his office, waving toward a chair, then hung up his coat and went to the dirty window where the view of Chicago was restricted to one traffic-clogged street. He watched as cab drivers made kamikaze assaults on the turn lane and everyone else played bumper tag.

After the traffic light changed to red for the third time, Riordan said, "Three teams, Frank. You're responsible for thirty men. I expected you to put your unit on the map. Last year your arrest record increased by only eight percent. And now this screw-up with Cantor. When a narc goes down he's supposed to be a hero. You don't even know why in the hell he was there. You know what it took to keep this under wraps? I expect more from you, Frank. Don't disappoint me like this again."

"Sorry, Sir."

Murphy sounded apprehensive. Riordan smiled. Leotha Jamison was in charge of Cantor's team. He wanted her out of Narcotics. She was in over her head, never should have gotten a promotion, or this assignment, and wouldn't have if Harold Washington hadn't been mayor. "I want Sergeant Jamison named in the internal investigation."

"Yes, Sir."

Turning, Riordan could see by the expression on Murphy's face that he hadn't expected to get off so easily, with just one head on the plate, and that head not his.

It was after nine when Riordan called it a night. The temperature had dropped below zero. He drove several blocks in the direction of the condo he had shared with his soon-to-be ex-wife before making an illegal U-turn and heading north. His apartment was too small. He hated to go there. He'd have to find a bigger place. He didn't like to be that confined.

As he had done so often lately, Riordan took LaSalle Street across the Chicago River to North. The lights were on in Dan's office. Riordan continued down the block, past the parking garage. For a moment he wondered what it would be like to fall from a roof and see the sidewalk rushing toward you. Nobody had heard Cantor scream.

Riordan picked up a pizza and circled back to Dan's place. The night guard nodded to him as he walked to the elevators. It was an old building with marble floors and columns and carved oak panelling on the walls. There was talk of tearing it down. Daniel Crosby and Associates was on the sixth floor.

Dan was alone. Riordan followed him down a hall with offices on both sides to a large room with thick double doors. After Dan retired from the department three years ago, this place had become his home. The sofa converted to a bed; cabinets concealed a refrigerator, freezer, and microwave oven, stereo equipment, and a wide-screen TV. A stationary bike was set up in the corner. Crosby needed to use it, Riordan thought. He was really out of shape.

Riordan put the pizza on a table by the window and looked down at two commuters huddled in a bus kiosk, a few scurrying pedestrians, the inevitable traffic.

"All you need here, Dan, is a view."

"Even without one, this is a long way from Bridgeport."

How many times had they said that? They had grown up in the old neighborhood, lived next door to each other in identical bungalows, watched their mothers arrange geraniums on the front steps and plant marigolds in windowboxes, helped their fathers mow narrow strips of grass. They had walked the same two blocks to St. Columbine's, where they were scolded by the same nuns. Dan, four years older, had preceded him on the force, where they both knew they'd go, just as their fathers and grandfathers and several uncles before them. Sometimes the predictability of his life made Riordan restless, but not enough to change anything except wives. Margo was his third. There would probably be another. He liked having a woman around.

"You've gotta get out more, Joe. Leave the job for a couple of hours, stop brooding over Margo. You promised me you'd come over last night. What happened?"

"I got tied up."

"Yeah. That happens a lot. I remember, and I'm glad it's behind me. This is better, much better."

Dan sounded like an old man. Hell, Dan was beginning to look old. He was getting stooped shouldered like his father, and his hair was gray. He was moving slower these days and getting forgetful.

"Whenever you're ready, Joey, I've got a place for you right here."

Dan had preceded him in everything, from altar boy at St. Collie's to football captain in high school to vice deputy. Now Dan wanted him to take early retirement, but Riordan had no intention of ever investigating things like insurance fraud. As much as he preferred a desk to walking a beat, he couldn't work in an office that didn't have a direct line to the action. At the rate Dan was going, the only action in this place in a couple of years would be an afternoon nap. Besides, there was still one thing he could do that Dan couldn't—become superintendent.

Dan put a six pack of beer on the table and opened the pizza box. "Remember old man Martinelli throwing the pizza dough up in the air and catching it on his fists? And that sauce his old lady made. Now we gotta settle for this, cardboard smeared with catsup."

He took paper plates and napkins from a cabinet. "I didn't see nothin' about Cantor in the paper this morning but his obit."

"With luck, that's all you'll read."

"Good work. You called Feldman at the *Trib* like I told you?"

"Great guy, Feldman," Riordan said. He had his own contacts now.

"You still don't know what went down?"

"No, but Cantor's sergeant is under investigation."

"Smart move, Joe. These damned quotas have got the department all screwed up. Jamison only scored ninety-four on the exam. A lot of guys must have scored higher. You'd think with a hundred and ten slots to be filled from a field of twenty-five hundred, that they'd be more selective. This affirmative-action crap about 'most qualified' being anybody who scores in the ninetieth percentile is bullshit. Too bad about Cantor, though."

"Yeah," Riordan said.

"What have you got so far?"

Once a cop, always a cop. Dan wanted all of the details, but Riordan had been up most of the night before and was too tired to fill him in.

"You don't know what happened up there, huh?"

"Not yet."

"Cantor was damned good undercover. I tell you about the time he set up a bust on a couple of broads he went to school with and they never knew it was him?"

"Yeah." If he had, Riordan didn't remember.

"Hey, you thought about replacing him yet? There's this kid from the old neighborhood, his uncle was a cop . . . "

Riordan chewed on a mouthful of pepperoni and mozzarella and washed it down with some beer. "I'll take a look at him, Dan, but you gotta cut out trying to do my job for me. I'm not doing too bad." He had filled the fifty slots that were vacant in his department when Dan retired, and replaced fifteen other cops who had transferred out or retired.

"I'm telling you, Joey, this kid is sharp. Works out of the sixth district. Murphy's not putting out like you expected, and with Cantor's death, he might have to go." Dan had recommended Murphy, not that he would admit it now.

"Not yet," Riordan said, although he was beginning to agree. Arrests had increased by twenty-one percent since Riordan had been in charge; the conviction rate increased by seventeen percent. Murphy's unit was operating well below that level. Things would slip even more without Cantor.

For a moment he thought of Rachel Cantor. "What are you covering up now?" she had asked. Did Cantor tell her that he heard someone drop Johnny MacAlister's name? Did Cantor tell her who said it? He didn't think so. Rachel Cantor was angry enough to have said something if she knew.

Dan turned off the lights and stood at the window, watching as Joe Riordan stepped out into the swirling snow and crossed the street. Joey had done a lot better than he thought he would when Dan recommended him to take over his department. Of course that was because he had hand picked most of Riordan's Raiders before Joey took over. Now there was talk of Joey becoming superintendent, but Joey had a real Achilles' heel when it came to personnel. Sooner or later it would catch up.

Sitting behind a desk and running the show wasn't Joey's strong suit either, Dan thought. He belonged on the street. It was getting to him, being so far from the action, but there was no going back. Joey was getting cocky, let a little luck go to his head. He hadn't gotten burned yet, so he wasn't ready to think about retiring. Too bad. If he did, they could spend more time at his cabin in Wisconsin, and now that he'd bought a condo in Florida, there was deep-sea fishing and scuba diving, too. Joey was always too busy to go hunting and swimming and fishing like they did in the old days.

Wait till Joey found out he could fly an airplane. Fifty-eight lessons so far, and he was almost ready to solo. Hell, he could solo—the damned instructor was just milking him out of more money for lessons. But what the hell, he didn't really want to be up there alone. The instructor was good company. He liked having the kid in the cockpit. Now that he'd bought that Cherokee . . . that was going to be Joey's birthday present, a ride to the clouds, just the two of them. They could go up to Milwaukee, maybe. May fifth. It seemed like a long time to wait.

Maybe now that Joey was getting rid of Margo he'd want to get away for a few days. Joey's taste in women wasn't worth shit, not that Dan would ever say so. Maybe with this one sucking him dry, he'd figure it out.

A squad car drove through the slush. Dan felt a tightness in his chest as the squad slowed to observe two men standing in a doorway. Dan watched the man in the trench coat, half expecting to see his arm swing up with an AK-47 and blow the uniform away. In the fraction of a second that it took the squad to pick up speed and pass the two men, Dan's mouth got dry and his heartbeat increased. God, but he was glad to be out of it.

He had felt like a target every time he put on his uniform. His uncle the alderman had enough clout to get him into 11th and State in less than a year, but those ten months he spent walking a beat on State Street had been hell. Every job he had in the department brought its own kind of hell, but nothing was worse than the street. When that colored lady rear-ended him and he injured his back, he was so happy he saw to it that two of them from the old neighborhood got into the academy. Coloreds in Bridgeport, Mayor Daley's neighborhood—Who would have believed it? His old man must have turned over in his grave when the coloreds and the Puerto Ricans began moving in.

One man in the doorway passed something to the other. Both men started walking in opposite directions. He knew it, a buy. Tensing, he waited for the unmarked car to move in, but nothing happened. He thought about Julian Cantor and wondered if anyone kept track of his scores. Joey was right, Cantor had been a good narc, one of the best. His death was a big loss to the department. Damned shame he went out like he did. The man deserved something heroic.

Restless and wide awake, Dan moved about the room. He looked at the last slice of pizza. It was cold, but he ate it anyway. He'd go out for a while. A walk would help him sleep better. Crosby unlocked a cabinet, then a drawer where he kept his guns—seventeen, none registered, picked up while he was with the department. He chose one of the smaller, lighter pieces, a .38. The way the streets were now, he never felt safe.

3

Marti decided to take Thursday off. She had missed Julian Cantor's funeral yesterday, and she couldn't put off seeing Rachel any longer. There hadn't been a homicide in Lincoln Prairie for over a week, and her next court appearance was tomorrow. For a minute, she considered calling Rachel and using case preparation as an excuse to stay away. *Coward,* she chided herself. She told Vik where she was going, explaining only that a narc Johnny knew had died.

Marti took Green Bay Road as far as Highland Park, stopped at a kosher deli and picked up lox and bagels for the ten men who would sit shiva tonight. Anticipating delays due to construction on the Kennedy Expressway, she reached the northwest side of Chicago sooner than she expected. Her dread was old and familiar as she turned the corner and watched for the two-story brick building where Rachel lived.

Julian and Johnny didn't hang out together. Their families didn't socialize. They didn't work together. But through some bond, felt rather than spoken, they had become friends.

Marti pulled into a parking space three houses from the Cantors'. There weren't many other cars on the street, none with department plates. A tall black fence extended from the sides of the house to the middle of the sidewalk and protected the entrance. Marti rang the bell and waited until a voice spoke through the intercom.

"Who is it?" someone asked.

Marti identified herself.

After a moment the voice responded. "Come in. I am Rachel's aunt. She will see you."

An old woman, short and slender in a stylish black suit, opened the door. "It is good of you to come."

Inside, the rooms were airy and light, the furnishings expensive, with bric-a-brac scattered on tables and sideboards. Rachel's father owned a chain of furniture stores and the white, overstuffed chair in the living room reminded Marti of one she had seen on his most recent television commercial. The old woman reset the security system.

Rachel was upstairs in a sitting room at the rear of the house. Marti had forgotten how young she was, probably in her late twenties. Julian was forty-six. Short, dark curls framed Rachel's triangular face. She, too, was dressed in black, with a fringed shawl draped over her shoulders. There were circles under her eyes and she had been crying.

"Marti, I was hoping you would come."

They sat by the window, watching as a squirrel slipped off an ice-covered tree branch, grabbing at the air as it fell into a pile of snow.

"This has been such a long winter," Rachel said, wringing her hands. "Such a long, bitter winter. Will this ever end?"

Marti thought of Johnny, so still, so stiff in the casket, not looking anything like himself. To hide the exit wound, the undertaker had covered Johnny's head with a kinky afro wig, helping her pretend for just a little while longer that it wasn't him.

"It gets better," she said.

Rachel searched Marti's face, then shook her head. "But it doesn't end."

When Marti didn't answer, Rachel said, "You moved away."

"I couldn't . . . function here," Marti admitted. One night, about a month after Johnny died, while she was on patrol, she . . . Marti pressed her fingertips to her temples. Even now she couldn't bring herself to think about it. "One night I met myself in an alley," she said. The next morning, she put the house up for sale.

"You took it with you, though, didn't you?"

"Some things don't go away. I stopped . . . waiting, after I left here."

Rachel pulled her shawl tighter. "Waiting. I know. I saw so little of Julian since Hanukkah. He would come in at such odd hours. And it seemed like I was always waiting for him to come home . . . Even now I wait. As if he isn't . . ."

Her fingers dug into the shawl. "How long will I listen for the phone to ring, for footsteps on the stairs, for water running in the shower? How long will I wait for him to come home?"

Marti stared out the window. The squirrel was climbing the branch again. Or maybe it was a different squirrel. Climbing, sliding, climbing. "Forever," she said. "I think you wait forever."

Rachel poked her finger through the shawl. "But it gets better?"

"Yes, it does."

A dog padded into the room, glanced at Marti and went to Rachel, nudging her hand. Childless after seven or eight years of marriage, Rachel raised show dogs. Marti couldn't identify the breed. It was tan and white, with short hair, short legs and big pointy ears. It seemed out of proportion.

"Yusef is a Corgi," Rachel said. "They're dwarfs." She kept stroking the dog's fur. "Julian was undercover on this job for a long time. He said it was almost over, that he'd just do routine busts for a while when it was. I always felt safer with him way undercover like that, though, because he was so damned good at becoming whoever he was supposed to be. I thought he was safer than when he was on a buy team, or going through doors." The dog leaned closer. "I thought he was safer. I went to sleep that night thinking he was safe. How could I . . ."

As Rachel spoke, Marti remembered being with the other wives when Johnny died, with other cops, with her partner, with Momma. She had never told anyone how she felt, not even Momma. Had one of those wives lost a husband, too? Could one of them have said something that would have helped?

"How long is it before you can sleep without dreaming, Marti? Do the nightmares stop?"

She had dreamed she was on the firing range, then Johnny became the target and she woke up, drenched in sweat. She had forgotten about the dreams. How could she forget something like that? "The nightmares go away," she said. But even now she woke up sweating sometimes, unable to remember what she had dreamed.

"It just takes time, Rachel. You have to give it time." Her stomach felt like someone was kneading it. She was getting nauseous. She shouldn't have come here. She couldn't be of any help to Rachel. It was too upsetting, reliving the past.

"I can't tell you anything good," Marti said. "You don't ever forget. There's always something unsaid. Maybe it's good-bye, I don't know. You want them to come home but you know they aren't going to. You stop getting angry every time you remember all the things you were going to do together some day." She was squeezing her hands so tight they hurt. "You stop being angry with him for leaving you. You stop regretting things you said, things you didn't say, because you know he must be someplace where he knows all of that. But I don't think you ever stop wanting to . . . see him . . . one more time . . . just one more time."

Marti wiped her eyes. She would not cry.

Rachel leaned forward. "Thank you," she said, patting Marti's hand. "I thought I was going crazy."

"You are, in a way," Marti said. She knew this would be the most insane period of Rachel's life. "But . . . "

"I know." Rachel sniffled and blew her nose. "It gets better."

She seemed calmer when she spoke again. "Do you believe what they told you after it happened?"

Marti hesitated. "I don't want to believe it."

"Why not?"

"Because . . . I knew him."

"And I knew Julian. Riordan tried to say he got careless, and then, when I didn't agree, that Julian might have had personal reasons, that it could have been deliberate. Julian didn't go over the edge of that roof accidentally or deliberately, Marti. He was pushed."

Marti wanted to remind Rachel of what it took to be a narc—overconfidence, belief in your own invincibility. But she had just begun to deal with that herself. Better to listen.

"I know how you feel."

"This operation was different, Marti. Julian went deeper undercover than he ever had before. He was on this assignment for two months. Sometimes he was gone for over a week. And it was big, it was something really big. He couldn't wait to get back out there. Marti, I think something happened. I think something went wrong when they made the buy or the bust or whatever. I think Riordan's covering something up."

"Did Julian talk to you about the job?"

"He didn't tell me everything, but most of the time I knew a lot about what he was doing. Not this time, though. But he was . . . excited. You know how they get sometimes. And now . . . Marti, I don't believe what they're telling me. If something went wrong, then Julian died in the line of duty. He died being a cop. He lived to be a cop, Marti. He would have been on the force twenty-five years in September. It's not fair that they should get away with a lie."

"Maybe they're not lying."

"Do you believe what they told you about Johnny?"

Marti shook her head. "But—"

"No. No buts, Marti. You knew Johnny as well as I knew Julian. They don't know more about our husbands than we do. We can't let them make us believe that they do."

"Rachel, being a narc, it's different."

"Oh, I know how it is. They love the danger. They think they're immortal. I know Julian was convinced nothing could possibly happen to him when he went to the roof of that parking garage. But something did. And they're not telling the truth about it. And that's what happened with Johnny."

Maybe. Marti sighed. She didn't want to think about the possibilities.

"Marti, a week ago, when Julian called home, he told me someone had dropped Johnny's name."

Marti felt a sudden thudding in her chest. Was Rachel telling her this because she wanted her to get involved in finding out what happened to Julian? Or was it the truth?

"Who?" she asked.

"I have no idea. You know how those things are. It's been

almost three years, something was bound to surface sooner or later. Julian didn't make a big deal of it. He said it could take months for something to come of it, if anything ever did."

"It could have been anything, anyone," Marti agreed.

"But Julian jumping off a roof sounds as crazy as what happened to Johnny. Our husbands are dead, Marti. There are no medals, no commendations, no hero's funeral, and hardly even an obituary. Everything was kept quiet. And neither of us believes what the department has told us. You, you're a cop. Didn't you ever try to find out? Didn't you ever want to?"

Again, Marti thought of that night in the alley. The night she wanted to beat that perp senseless. She hadn't known how angry she was until that kid spit at her and she grabbed him and forced him over the hood of that car and her partner talked her down.

"You're where I was, Rachel. Could you?"

Rachel thought for a moment, then shook her head. "I don't even know how I'm going to deal with tonight. How I'm going to get up in the morning."

"That's how it was for me."

Instead of returning to Lincoln Prairie, Marti drove to Ashland Avenue and took that to Roosevelt Road. She turned right, drove three blocks, then turned left, heading south until she reached the street where she grew up. Forty-seven years ago, her parents had come here from Arkansas. Now Momma had returned there and the house they had bought here was torn down. In the weed-filled lot where the house had stood, five middle-aged men gathered around a fire in a steel drum and passed a bottle.

Across the street, half a dozen boys, none of them over ten, sat on the crumbling concrete steps of a burned-out red-brick building where Johnny used to live. They were sharing a joint. The colors of their caps announced their gang affiliation and the angle of the visors dared rival members to approach.

Years ago, Marti attended the school just down the street, went to church just two blocks over. In the morning, sometimes before daybreak, the women who did days' work in Winnetka and Lake Forest would leave home, their bags bulging with a change of clothes. They would wear comfortable shoes worn down at the heels and laugh as they called to one another while they walked to the el. Soon those who didn't work as far away would head for the buses. The women who remained became surrogate parents. Miss Cora took care of Marti and her brother, Nathaniel, before and after school because her parents worked for the railroad. Daddy was a porter and away from home a lot. Momma cleaned the trains.

After school and on Saturdays, they would toss buckets full of hot, soapy water on the stairs and sweep the water across the sidewalk to the gutter. They would plant marigolds and petunias in the small patches of hard earth on either side of the stairs and pick green tomatoes from plants that grew along the south side of the house. Summer seemed to last forever, sunny and hot with quick, drenching thunderstorms. And winter, with deep snow and icy winds, kept them inside with cups of cocoa and oatmeal cookies while they listened to "Gas Light" and "The Shadow" on the radio.

Now a pack of dogs snapped and snarled as they fought for position on the icy sidewalk and attacked a mound of garbage. Marti slowed as two teenaged girls sauntered across the street. One of them flipped her the finger and mouthed the word "bitch."

She had drawn hopscotch squares on this street, played double-dutch and Red Light, and walked Johnny to the corner store. At night they would have talent shows on Johnny's roof. Coming here now was like returning to a war zone. What had happened to home?

"Drugs," Johnny had said, long before anyone else thought it was a problem. "Drugs," he repeated as the street began claiming their friends. "Drugs," he muttered, hitting the palm of his hand with his fist when he told her that his sister was gone.

Whatever happened the night that Johnny died, he was out there because he believed that he had to do something to stop the drugs. They both knew that nothing would ever change this neighborhood and bring back what once was. But he had to do what he could. Even if he had gotten careless or, for a moment, forgot that he wasn't invincible, nobody in the department had acknowledged that commitment. And she had failed him, and failed her children, by allowing them to deny him that. Whether or not Julian Cantor had heard somebody talking about Johnny's death, she was going to have to find out what happened, and why. Marti was gripped by a familiar reluctance. Before that could deter her, she pulled into a filling station and used the pay phone to call Johnny's old partner, DaVon Holmes.

4

It was after nine o'clock Thursday night when Marti parked at a beach in Evanston near the Northwestern University campus. Piles of snow partially obstructed her view of the lake. It was so dark she could hardly tell where the water ended and the sky began. Far in the distance, a buoy with blinking lights dipped and bobbed. The place was deserted, the street and nearest building a good fifty yards away. Uneasy, she reversed the car so that the bumper almost touched the snowbank and the car hood faced the street. She kept the engine running and thought about what she was going to say.

She had never spoken to DaVon at any length about the night Johnny died. What he had said at the time confirmed her own impressions. Johnny hadn't seemed depressed about anything, although he did seem preoccupied. There was nothing unusual about Johnny's attitude, nothing different about his behavior. She had repeated that to Joe Riordan, who was Johnny's lieutenant then, as well as to Dan Crosby, who had been commander of the Narcotics Division, but because there were no witnesses, there was nothing else to be done.

After about five minutes, an old Dodge pulled up beside her. One fender was peeled back, exposing part of the wheel, and a sheet of plastic replaced a side window. When DaVon got out, Marti could tell it was him by his eyes. The lower half of his face was hidden by a scarf and a hat was pulled down over his forehead and ears. His jacket, dark and nondescript, was torn at the shoulder and splattered with paint.

She unlocked the door on the passenger side. "How's things?"

"Great. Just great." DaVon's teeth were chattering.

She put the fan on high and shifted away from the heat vents as hot air blew on her legs. "Coffee?" She had brought a thermos.

"Great. That pile of junk's got no heater."

At DaVon's request, Marti had borrowed a car that was impounded. His vehicle looked more like something salvaged from a junkyard.

"Night off?" she asked.

"No, I'm on surveillance. Worked a straight nine-to-five today. How anyone could do that day after day beats the hell outta me. A couple years of that clock-watching shit and I'd be locked up. My old man did it for thirty-five years. Got up at four-thirty every morning and worked the steel mills in Gary. Dropped dead six months after he retired. Nothin' else to live for. I don't know how he did it. I'd go nuts."

DaVon gulped at the coffee, then slouched down in the seat as if he was concerned about being seen.

"You worried that I'll blow your cover? I can drive someplace else."

"No. No. Force of habit."

Johnny always said it was impossible to ever feel safe working undercover.

DaVon coughed. "Can't shake this cold. Damn winter's gonna last forever. It ain't been warm since October. Snow'll be here till May."

He was talking too much, really wired.

"So how do you like it, Marti? Life in the suburbs. Couldn't handle it, myself. Not near enough action. I can just see me taking someone in for smokin' a joint. Made a major bust last week. I was manning the ram and the suckers were so happy when we ran in screaming 'Police!' that they never went for their weapons. Place down the street had gotten busted by some Colombian dealers the week before. They killed everybody, even a couple of kids. I thought those guys were gonna thank us for being cops, they were so friendly. Damned shame to be that scared of the competition.

"That place was armed like a fortress. Uzis, AK-37s, you name it. And they were livin' high. New furniture, forty-six-inch TV. And roaches everywhere. Half hour after I left the place a roach crawled out of my sleeve and I'd hung my coat on a light fixture." He shook his head. "God, that place was filthy. All that fancy stuff and fifty thousand dollars stuffed in a drain pipe, and they lived like pigs.

"Had five little kids crawling around in there. Fat butts, all of them. The dealer had rigged some diapers to hold his shit and he'd just made a buy. Each of them kids musta been wearing a couple pounds of cocaine."

Marti poured more coffee. She felt hot and unbuttoned her coat.

"How are Theo and Joanna?" DaVon asked.

"Okay. It still gets rough this time of year, but they're doing okay."

"And you?"

"I'm all right."

"Seeing anyone?"

"No. Not really."

"Johnny wouldn't want you to be by yourself. We talked about it sometimes."

"Oh?" Partners talked about a lot of things. She was counting on that.

"Yeah. He, um, he thought it might be hard for you, you two knew each other so long. Strange guy, Johnny. Woman goes by, we look. We all look. But him, I don't think he ever did. Nobody ever teased him about it, though." He covered his mouth, coughing. "We figured you'd beat up on him if he messed around."

She smiled. Johnny was a leg man. He had looked at a lot of women's legs. "What were you talking about that night?"

DaVon sucked in his breath and hesitated. "He was talkin' about Joanna. They'd gone to that father and daughter dinner your church had, and he was talkin' about her going to her first prom in a coupla years. I teased him about thinking like an old man. He said, 'Maybe I won't get to see her.' "

Marti gripped the steering wheel. Johnny and Joanna had been so happy that night, him in his best suit and Joanna in that mint-green dress she had insisted on wearing to the wake and the funeral. "Is that all you talked about?"

"We were pretty focused on the buy. And we were getting ready to set up another surveillance. We had just got a tip from a snitch. You know, the job."

"He went into that cemetery alone."

"I was backing him up."

"Why did he go in there?"

"He wanted to talk to a snitch. You know how that is."

Snitches were open game if it became known that they were giving information to the cops. Their identity was one of the few secrets partners might keep from each other.

"Johnny went behind a mausoleum. I was sitting under a tree. I didn't like the location. But Johnny, he really wanted to meet with this snitch, kept checking the time."

Marti wiped sweat from her forehead. The car was too hot. Her armpits were damp. She turned down the fan.

"I didn't see anyone go in or out. Johnny said it would take twenty minutes."

"Why was he seeing the snitch?"

"I don't know."

She wanted to believe him, but Johnny should have told him that much.

"What do you know?"

"Not enough. I can't help you." He said that with less conviction.

"Try, DaVon." Something had been worrying Johnny those last few weeks. He didn't talk with her about the job very often, but she should have asked what it was. Maybe he would have told her.

"Why couldn't you see anything?"

"I was on the other side of that mausoleum. I told Johnny it wasn't a good location and he agreed. But the snitch wouldn't meet him anyplace else."

"Were you going to do anything different that night?"

"Nothing. Routine buys, if we could score. Nothing we hadn't done dozens of times."

She had tried to think things through, figure out what was different about that night. There had to be something DaVon wasn't telling her. Maybe he didn't even think it was important.

She didn't know enough to ask the right questions. "Was this one of his regular informants?"

"As far as I know. He would have mentioned it if it was somebody new. You know how Johnny was. A lot of the time he was real quiet."

"You were his partner. If he had something on his mind—"

"Right. I like to think he would have told me, too. But he didn't. And then he was . . . gone. That was hard, Marti. Hard for me, not just you. We rode together for two years, but I wasn't there for him that night. I wasn't there. He was in there eighteen minutes when I heard the shot . . . and I wasn't that far away. It was too late. And . . . I didn't see anybody. I looked, but I didn't see anybody."

Marti squeezed his hand. There was no comfort for that, not for a cop. "It's okay. I understand."

"Well, I don't. And it's a bitch trying to live with it."

She'd run away, left the department, left town. DaVon had stayed, dealt with it. "Do you believe it was an accident? Or that it was suicide?"

"I don't see how it could have been either. I told them that. I wasn't there. I couldn't prove anyone else had been there. I told them that."

"Someone dropped Johnny's name a week or so ago."

He seemed surprised. "Who?"

"I don't know."

"What'd they say?"

"I don't know that either."

She waited, then said, "Have you heard anything?"

"No."

"If you did, would you tell me?"

"If I did, I'd check it out myself first. Johnny was my partner. I owe him. I owe you."

"Remember that, if you hear anything."

She opened both windows as soon as DaVon got out, welcoming the cold blast of air. Then she thought of the question she hadn't asked. If Johnny had made a mistake. If he had done or said something he shouldn't have. If he had gotten cocky, or careless, or if he'd gotten so addicted to the high that he ignored caution.

DaVon watched as Marti's car pulled out of the parking lot, staring until he couldn't see the taillights anymore. He shivered, sitting in the cold, remembering what had happened almost three years ago. He and Johnny hadn't been best friends or drinking buddies. When their watch was over, Johnny always went home. But they had been partners.

Johnny did go in there to see a snitch. He said it had something to do with a bust they made over a year ago. He said he couldn't talk about it, but he would if he had to go to Internal Affairs. With all the shit they were into . . . Johnny never did like the way they were running their investigations, but the most trouble they could have gotten into would have been to make Crosby mad, and Crosby couldn't have done shit about it without screwing himself.

When Johnny went down, DaVon had told them that he was too far away. Then the reports went missing. Three days later, when they asked him for another statement, he changed some of it. The parts that made him negligent. By then Riordan had talked to him. He'd said it was for the good of the unit. But now . . . he was going to have to do something. Make amends, his AA sponsor said. Amends. Tell them that he got careless, that he was too far away, that he should have moved in closer once Johnny was on the other side of that mausoleum. Tell them how much time elapsed from when he heard the gunshots until he reached Johnny.

Amends. AA. He couldn't stay out of the bottle long enough last week to make it to a meeting. This week he had to stay dry. Was he going to be able to stay dry long enough to get the job done? How long before he was drinking then, too? He wanted a drink right now. Especially now, having seen Marti. He should have told her something, but what? He didn't know enough to tell anyone yet. He did know Johnny cultivated a snitch named Fayesta not long before he went down. And he'd find out what they talked about.

Saturday. Two more days until this bust went down. Then he'd find out what Johnny knew. Was that what it would take to stay dry? Jesus, how he wanted to get out of the bottle, get his life back, his kids.

DaVon shivered again, remembering. Johnny said he'd be out in twenty minutes. He was farther away than he should have been. But Johnny was always so sure of himself. Johnny could talk to anybody, talk his way out of anything. Johnny was the smoothest talking . . . Twenty minutes, Johnny said, give me twenty minutes. Won't take no longer than that. Habit made DaVon keep checking his watch. Eight minutes and the shot was fired. As soon as the gun went off he was running, but there was too much time between them.

He was all the back-up that Johnny had, and he was too late. He was the one who got careless. He was the one who was so damned confident in what Johnny could do, and when Johnny couldn't quite pull it off . . . Now, there was nothing anyone could do. And now, every day, he had to live with it.

5

After court on Friday, Marti and Vik went to the Barrister, a pub not far from the precinct. Brass fixtures, dark panelling, a dart board, and stained-glass swag lamps made the place seem cozy.

"Well, MacAlister, two for us and zip for Attorney Allen."

"That's easy for you to say, you were only on the stand for ten minutes." Marti leaned back in the booth and closed her eyes. Her testimony had taken all morning. "I could sit here for the rest of the day without moving. Maybe you were more intimidating."

At six two, Vik was four inches taller than Marti. There was a suggestion of ferocity in his narrow face. His beak nose was bent from a break, there were always dark pouches under his eyes, and wiry salt-and-pepper eyebrows curled in all directions. At forty-nine, Vik was the senior man on a youthful force, but few dared to call him old.

"I think Allen thought he would have an easier time with you," Vik said. "Slick suburban attorney makes the dumb, big-city cop look bad. I guess we showed him. All that time we put in yesterday sure paid off."

Allen, the defense attorney, loved to discredit expert witnesses by asking a seemingly innocuous yes-or-no question about one bit of evidence and following that with a dozen more questions that became increasingly convoluted.

"I had a hell of a time trying to follow him after a while," Marti said. "I wonder how long it takes him to think up questions like that."

"Did you see how answering him with a summary of every detail ticked him off?"

"Good strategy, but I just didn't want to give him any loopholes. By the time he stopped talking I wasn't always sure what he'd asked. And when I asked him to repeat it, it got worse."

"Well, the state's attorney loved every minute of it, once she saw you could handle him. I even think the judge was impressed. He overruled all of Allen's objections."

The waitress came over to their table with her pen poised. Marti shook her head. Vik looked at her with furrowed brows, then ordered a sandwich. "We'll both have coffee," he added.

When the waitress turned away, he said, "Damned shame about that cop you were telling me about."

"Julian Cantor."

"I don't think there was anything in the newspaper. I didn't even notice an obit. What happened?"

"He went over a ledge at the parking garage at University of Chicago Medical Center."

"Accidentally or on purpose?"

"Depends on who you talk to." She looked out the window. It was snowing again. "The department isn't saying much of anything. His wife thinks somebody helped him."

"How well did you know him?"

"Not really. Johnny did." She couldn't recall anything Johnny had said about Julian except "catbird," which meant that Julian never allowed himself to be placed at a disadvantage. Julian must have done just that the night he died. "He was a narc. He and Johnny didn't work together as far as I know, but they were friends. Nothing social. Just friends."

"Is this what's been on your mind the past few days?" Vik asked.

The waitress brought Vik's Reuben and two cups of hot coffee. Vik reached for the sugar. "You've been real quiet."

Marti stirred her coffee until the sound of the spoon scraping against the cup became annoying. "Rachel Cantor says Julian heard someone drop Johnny's name about a week before he died."

"What does that mean?"

"Maybe nothing. Or, maybe someone knows something and it's beginning to get to them."

"What do you think?"

"I think I have to find out what happened. Not knowing . . . we can't seem to let go. Everything becomes such a hurdle. We get past one thing, like Joanna dating, and then it's Theo running out on the basketball court for the first time." Johnny had gone to Northern Illinois on a basketball scholarship. She had put Johnny's trophies in storage. Should she get them out? Would that make things worse? "I try, but I'm never sure what I should do."

Marti ran her fingers through her hair. "Other families, they have something—their dad's star in the hero case at Eleventh and State, the medal, the story about how brave he was, something. We just . . . before, I worried that Theo did well in school because his father always excelled and he thought he had to live up to that. Now I worry that he's not doing well because he thinks his father was a failure, or a quitter, or maybe that his father didn't care about him, about us. Johnny loved his children. I don't want anything to get in the way of their knowing that."

Neither of them spoke for a few seconds. "Are you going to try to find out what happened?" Vik said.

"We need to know."

She looked outside again, trying to absorb some of the tranquility of the snow coming down in tiny flakes.

"I talked to Johnny's old partner last night. He said the same thing as before, that Johnny was supposed to be meeting a snitch, that he wasn't in a good location as back-up. I think he might have been holding back, but when your partner goes down, and you're all the back-up he has . . . you must block some of it out."

"What do you think happened?" Vik asked.

"I think . . . " She took a deep breath. "Overconfidence." Saying it made her throat hurt.

"What are we going to do?" Vik asked.

Marti looked at him, remembering her first day on the job. "Man's work, policing," Vik had told her. "We don't let anything as unreliable as intuition interfere with common sense and sound judgment." Vik smoked then. One long drag on his cigarette and a quick flick of his finger as he knocked off the ash dismissed her ten years on the force and four commendations in Chicago.

"We?" Marti said. She squeezed his hand. "You haven't touched your sandwich."

"Does this mean we'll have to go to Chicago?"

Marti smiled. "How long have you harbored this secret desire to be a big-city cop?"

Vik munched on a pickle. "I'm serious. We're partners. I'm in."

"You're in," Marti agreed. "Partner. But I'm not sure what I'm going to do yet. And don't get your hopes up. The odds on car chases, getting shot at, and political intrigue are slim."

Reaching for his sandwich, Vik smiled.

C H A P T E R

6

DaVon was whistling as he parked the van alongside a U-shaped apartment building Saturday morning. Gang signs and graffiti were sprayed on the red brick. Cardboard replaced many of the window panes, with rags stuffed in smaller breaks. Curtains, sheets, even clothing had been hung in the windows to keep out the cold and the wind. On the second floor, plywood hid the vertical bars that protected four windows. Inside, DaVon knew *that* apartment had metal doors with bars to prevent entry. The occupants were armed. Drug dealers. If they noticed his van, they might be glad he was here—the lettering on the van said Able Heating and Plumbing. The furnace that heated this section of the building hadn't worked in four days. DaVon had been tipped off to a major buy that was supposed to go down here soon and had parked here for three days to observe the action while a team of officers inside pretended to fix the furnace.

DaVon covered his mouth as he coughed. He couldn't keep warm, even with three layers of clothes. He couldn't keep the engine running—it would draw too much attention, even though folks would expect someone to stay with the van to keep stuff from getting ripped off. If he could just shake this damned cold. He hadn't felt good in a week. After they made this bust he'd take a couple days off, get some rest, find out who Johnny's snitch was and what the hell was going on.

He watched the street, reporting to the three other cops inside the van. Jim would remain inside, coordinating communication, monitoring everyone's wire. The other two would go to the basement. Then they would wait. Two more cops were in an empty apartment down the hall from their mark. When they were ready to go in, more cops would come. DaVon had got lucky again and drawn the short straw. He would be on the team that manned the ram. He rubbed his gloved hands together, as much in anticipation as from the cold. There was nothing like feeling that door give way and being the first man in.

"Nobody out here who looks interesting," DaVon said. "Just a couple of winos." Two days of surveillance seemed like a long time. It should pay off today. "Here comes that whore with the blonde streaks in her hair. Oops, mama done turned her first trick of the day. It ain't ten o'clock and she's already lookin' to score some shit. Wonder how many hits she'll cop today?"

Jim laughed. "Might not be enough blow-jobs out there to keep her in shit, cold as it is."

DaVon pulled his cap closer to his eyebrows and pulled his scarf over his mouth. Not that a hooker in search of a fix would notice anything less than a black-and-white parked near her supply.

A few minutes later a small boy turned the corner. "Hey, Jimbo, you got a picture of little dude here?"

"Got him yesterday and the day before."

DaVon took his gloves off to light a cigarette. "Sure bet he's dealing some of what he's buying at school."

The kid looked right at him, then went into the building. The other two cops in the back got out, lugging tool boxes filled with weapons to a side door that would take them to the cellar. He didn't envy them. It would be cold inside, too. Cold, damp, rat-and roach-infested. He shivered, then looked at the boarded-up windows. One less dealer, he reminded himself. One down, two hundred thousand to go.

DaVon finished off his cigarette with several deep drags and ground the butt into the floor of the van. "Here's grandma," he said as an old woman walked past. "Walkin' spry this morning. Be loaded down with shit when she comes out."

Behind him, Jim said, "Looks like business as usual. They musta got that shipment last night."

"Musta," DaVon agreed. They had worked with this snitch before. "Looks like good old Reena was right on the money again."

Three gang members went inside. "Those aren't the same dudes from yesterday or the day before. And so far that tall one's made the buys. They better not be comin' to rip this dude off. We're gettin' him today."

Jim spoke with the officers inside the building.

DaVon laughed. "Here comes Louie. He goes under damned near as good as . . . " He almost said Johnny. "About as good as anyone I've ever seen. Looks just like a junkie."

Jim told Louie about the gang members. When Louie came out of the building, he walked past the van and spoke into his wire. "Got some good shit in there today. Kingsmen makin' a major buy."

They waited. If their snitch was right, there was a whole lot of shit upstairs, and their mark was going to sell quite a few kilos to a suburban dealer today. The gang members came out, coats bulging.

After they turned the corner, DaVon rolled down the window to spit. "Bad when the air outside don't feel colder than the air inside," he said. He could switch on the engine for a few minutes, but that wouldn't do much good. Getting someone to go in and fool with the furnace had seemed like a good idea, and their cover was working, but damn.

"We're gonna have to come up with something really clever next time, Jimbo, and figure out a way to keep warm."

"Spring's coming."

DaVon rubbed at the condensation on the window. "Sure, you're right. Be spring before we know it."

He looked at the dirty mounds of snow and the thick icicles hanging from drainpipes and window ledges, and tried to recall what spring and warm weather were like. "Then the killings go up," he said.

He thought about Johnny again. Hard seeing Marti last night. Brought back too much that he needed to keep on forgetting. Who had repeated what he said? What did he say? He must have been drunk when he said it. Twenty minutes, Johnny had told him. Twenty minutes tops. Four to drive in, five out, ten max to talk with the snitch. But Johnny never came out.

DaVon stared at the dirty snow. "One thing about bad weather, it keeps a lot of folks in." Spring wouldn't bring nothing but trouble.

7

On Saturday afternoon, Marti met Theo and his friend Mike Walker, and Mike's dad, Ben, at a small museum on a forest preserve in Wauconda, about fifteen miles from Lincoln Prairie. The boys' Cub Scout den was studying Native American cultures and the boys had chosen the Potawatomi tribe.

Theo's teacher had called Marti last night. Theo had flunked this week's English and math tests, and in general was performing well below his ability. When Marti explained that the third anniversary of his father's death was approaching, Mr. Lambert didn't seem impressed. Annoyed, Marti suggested that perhaps she should discuss this with the principal. Mr. Lambert became more cooperative, agreeing to let Theo work on a math project as make-up, and also a report on the Potawatomi.

When Marti went into the kitchen, Sharon had spread out stacks of paper on the table.

"Looking at life through rose-colored glasses again?" Marti asked.

Sharon's square-framed spectacles were tinted pink.

"Some of these reports need more than that. I'm beginning to think I made a mistake, going from sixth grade to ninth. These kids needed me a few years ago. Some are really struggling now. And they don't seem to care anymore." She sighed, her face pensive. "February. I have worked so hard with my second-period class—" Sharon gestured toward one of the stacks—"and this is as far as they've come. Well, back to the drawing board." She pulled her glasses to the tip of her nose and looked over the rims. "What's with you?"

"Oh, nothing much. It's snowing again. I've got to take the car in for an oil change. Mr. Lambert called. Theo's flunking a few subjects. I was worried that he might become a compulsive over-achiever because that was how he remembered his father. I guess I shouldn't get so analytical. You do enough of that for both of us."

"In Theo's case, a few bad grades could be good. A little rebellion isn't always a bad thing."

"What if that was his way of . . . " Marti groped for words. "Joanna cooks all that natural food to keep me healthy, but Theo . . . "

"Theo was young enough when it happened to think that if he was very good, you wouldn't leave him the way Johnny did. Now he's old enough to wonder if he can trust you to stick around no matter what. Or, since kids are as complex as most other folks, maybe it's none of the above."

Still puzzled, Marti went to Theo's room. He had hardly touched his supper and was lying on his bed, playing with a hand-held electronic game he hardly ever bothered with. Marti sat near him and Bigfoot ambled over and nudge her hand. She rubbed the space between Bigfoot's ears until he sighed and laid down near her feet.

"I'm going to Joanna's game. She says you don't want to come."

"I've got homework."

"How are things going at school?"

"Mr. Lambert called, didn't he?"

"Some teachers don't care enough to call."

Theo pressed the buttons on the game and it made beeping sounds. In profile, he looked so much like his father—brown skin smooth as polished pecans, cleft chin, widow's peak—that Marti almost caught her breath. He was quiet like his father, too. But Marti had known Johnny for so long she could interpret most of his silences. Theo was often an enigma.

If Theo spoke of his father's death at all, it was in the completion of a model airplane he and Johnny had been working on when Johnny died, and a terrarium he made to remind him of the woods his father had shunned ever since he returned from Vietnam.

Theo was seven and a half when Johnny died. How much did he remember? Both children had nightmares that first year, fewer once they moved here. She told them the truth, that she didn't know how or why their father died. That the coroner ruled it accidental. That his lieutenant thought it might have been suicide.

Should she have told them that much? What if they had heard it from someone else? Should she have lied? Johnny wouldn't lie to them. She didn't think that she should either. It was harder, telling them the truth. Much harder helping them sort through what they knew about their father to arrive at their own conclusions. They said they didn't believe Johnny took his own life. But since nobody knew what happened . . .

"Is there anything special you think we should do April third?"

More beeps, then Theo shook his head. "It'll be too soon for the irises to come up."

Johnny's irises. Theo helped Johnny plant them in front of their house in Chicago. The three of them had transplanted some of the rhizomes at Johnny's grave.

"Do you remember helping your dad plant them?"

"I think so. Not really. I know I did."

"You picked out the yellow ones. And after they were planted, the two of you went out for pizza."

She stroked his hair, thick and kinky like Johnny's. "Theo, he did not want to leave you. He would want to be here."

After a moment, Theo said, "I know."

"And I'm not mad or upset about your grades. Which does not mean it's okay if it happens again."

"All right."

"I'd like it if you'd come to Joanna's game with me."

"Okay," he said, without enthusiasm.

When she reached the museum, Ben's van was in the parking lot. Sharon had introduced Marti to Ben. They weren't really dating but they did have the boys in common, and Ben's wife had died in a car accident about five years ago. It had been a few weeks since they last had dinner together, and she realized with a start that she had missed him. Ben was always so calm, and not just because of his training as a paramedic. Marti couldn't imagine Ben enjoying the thrill of a drug raid. Something about that was reassuring.

Three bicycles were attached to a rack on the back of the van. Ben had lost his wife when Mike was five. One of Ben's solutions to Mike's depression was exercise. Marti hoped biking had been good for both boys today.

A young Black man wearing a business suit was checking stock in the gift shop when Marti went inside. He came toward her, smiling.

"I'm Bill Rollins, visitor's services guide. Are you here with the two young men who are interested in local Native Americans? They asked me to watch for you." He led the way to a conference room. "Mr. Walker called ahead and I got out some things that aren't on display right now."

As she entered the room, Ben turned toward her and smiled. Ben was a large man, not fat, just big. He was about the same height as Johnny, but close to twenty pounds heavier. His caramel brown skin was creased with laugh lines at the corners of his eyes and mouth. He and the boys were wearing cloth gloves as they handled tools, arrowheads, and an assortment of bags, purses, and wallets.

"The Potawatomi were foragers," Bill Rollins explained, "so they moved around a lot. They used these to pack things in." He pointed to one of the larger bags. "This was made with rushes and grasses, and they used plant dyes. This"—he picked up what looked like miniature saddle bags—"this is early eighteenth century. The French brought glass beads, silver, and copper."

The geometric designs in the beadwork seemed to intrigue Theo. He looked and touched for a long time, then took photographs and wrote something in his notebook.

"I bet they liked moving around, and when they couldn't, they sat around making this stuff and talked about places they had been and where they were going," Theo said.

Mike, who was half a head shorter than Theo, round-faced and chubby, nodded. "It must have been cool around here back then, forests and bluffs, lots of animals. I bet it was a lot like it is up at Devil's Lake."

Marti looked closely at a small pouch. Although it didn't look fragile, it was so old she was afraid to handle it. It looked like something a woman would carry. The red, turquoise, and white beads were shiny against the tan animal skin. She looked away. The people who once needed these for travel were now confined to a reservation in Kansas. The woman who had made this was long dead.

"Would this have held something important?" Marti asked.

"No," the young man said. He pointed to some garments at the far end of the table. "Everything is like that—neckbands, arm bands, moccasins. Before they had beads they used porcupine quills colored with plant dyes, and stones and feathers. Incredible, isn't it, this need we have to create beauty?"

Marti watched as Theo puzzled over the bead designs. "They're perfect," he said. "There's not one mistake."

They moved on to a room filled with hands-on exhibits. While the boys explored the rest of the museum, Marti and Ben talked.

"Well," Ben said. "Theo seems temporarily distracted. He's been so depressed lately."

"How depressed? Worse than last year?" With anyone else except Sharon, Marti wouldn't have felt comfortable asking that about her own son. Ben understood that it wasn't because she was too busy to notice, but because Theo might behave differently when she wasn't around.

"I think so. Mike's been trying to get him to go out more, sledding, skating."

"I was hoping you'd tell me I was worrying too much."

"No. I've been concerned, too. I talked with the scout master about Webelos. We're going to come up with some special way to involve mothers, too. That way, Mike and Theo can help each other."

"Then it will be hard for Mike, too."

"He's going to have to work through something like that sooner or later. It seems easier for Joanna. Is it because she's older?"

"No. Not really. She missed all of her freshman dances because Johnny wasn't here to check out the boys who asked her."

"Then maybe, if Mike and Theo get through some of this together now, it'll be easier for them when they're her age."

"Maybe. And thanks. That's not something I would have thought of." She told him about her conversation with Mr. Lambert.

"I had a talk with him, too. In fact, I went to see him. We don't agree on a definition of masculinity, but he does understand that I'd rather have Mike deal with this and grow up than go through life with a lot of baggage that his mother wouldn't want him to carry around."

Marti shook her head. "This is the worst Theo's ever been. I'm going to try to spend more time with him, talk with him more, but when I'm working on a case . . ."

Ben brushed a strand of hair away from her face. "Theo will be all right. He can work through this. And he's got all of us."

As they were leaving, the boys spotted a flock of Canadian geese walking on a partially frozen pond. Toward the center, ducks swam in small circles.

"Stay away from the edge," Ben called as Theo and Mike ran toward the ice. He put his arm about Marti's waist and they walked to his van.

"I'm going to park a little nearer to the water," Ben said. "They need the fresh air, and lots more exercise." As they watched, the boys tried to coax the geese to come closer.

"You've been keeping yourself busy," Ben said.

"Just wrapped up a case a few days ago, and . . ." She told him about Julian Cantor's death and about Johnny's name surfacing.

"Are you doing okay?" Ben asked. "Another anniversary is coming up. You've got the kids to deal with. And now this."

"I'm okay."

"Sure. I've been there." Ben reached across the space between the seats and touched her hair. "See the pond?" he asked. "I love to look at the water. It's been here longer than anything else on earth. Be here when everything else is gone."

Ben put on a tape. As Marti listened to the music and watched Theo and Mike, for the first time in days she felt soothed.

8

It was after seven o'clock Saturday night when DaVon left the van. He didn't like going in after dark. It was easier to see each other in the daytime, but the suburban dealer who had just arrived preferred the night. As he made his way to the building, the air felt so cold his skin tingled. A block away, a car turned onto the street and he turned his face away from the glare of the headlights. He could feel his heart pounding and his breath was coming in quick gasps. He nodded to the cop who would man the ram with him. He was ready to go.

In the hallway, the smell of rotting wood and mildewed plaster was almost overwhelming. DaVon hugged the wall as he made his way past an overturned paper bag filled with garbage. Chicken bones and rice were scattered on the floor. Something was rummaging inside the bag. Please, no rats. No damned rats. Not now.

Near the stairwell, one dim bulb dangled from the ceiling on a long cord. The bannister felt slippery as he kept to the side of the stairs. There were no lights on the second floor. Rap music blared obscenities as his unit moved into position, weapons drawn. DaVon and Jimbo aimed the ram at the door.

Ten seconds and we'll be in, DaVon thought. Bile erupted in his mouth. He could smell his own sweat. He grinned and winked at Jimbo. It didn't get any better than this. Lieutenant Murphy gave the signal and they shouted "Police!"

Three hits and the door gave way. DaVon was running when he saw the bright flash. He never felt anything at all.

9

Marti drove into Chicago on Sunday. It was a little after two in the afternoon when she exited the Eisenhower Expressway and found a parking place near Leotha Jamison's condominium, not far from Austin Avenue and the city limits. Leotha had been Cantor's sergeant at the time of his death. She had seemed distracted on the phone, talking about DaVon's death one minute, Julian Cantor's the next, and then mentioning Johnny.

DaVon. Last night the blurb for the ten o'clock news, "Cop shot during drug raid," had set off a familiar churning in Marti's stomach even though she didn't know at first who it was, or how serious it was. She thought about her kids. Joanna and Sharon's daughter, Lisa, were at a party with their boyfriends and not likely to hear about it tonight. Theo was in bed. She would have to tell them first thing in the morning. Then she called a friend in Chicago. DaVon was dead. He went down while he was going through a door. Marti felt like someone had hit her in the gut with a brick. She rushed to the bathroom and threw up.

Leotha had called this morning, right after Marti got back from church. It was the mention of Johnny's name that brought her here. She didn't know Leotha that well, but Leotha had been a sergeant in Johnny's unit. They might have worked together.

Leotha came to the door in her bathrobe. Squinting, she shielded her eyes against the afternoon glare. She was as least ten years older than Marti, a couple of inches shorter and more slender. Light-skinned, with gray-green eyes, she was a shade lighter than Marti, what Momma would call high yellow.

"Glad you came, MacAlister." At a glance, she looked hung over, but Marti knew it was just lack of sleep. She probably didn't look much better herself—hadn't dozed off until almost four this morning.

Marti pushed aside the Sunday *Sun-Times* and the *Tribune* as she sat on the sofa, catching a glimpse of a DaVon's photograph on the front page.

"You okay?"

"No," Leotha said, cursing. "I'm not okay. I'm damned sure not okay."

She sat cross-legged in a chair across from Marti and lit a cigarette. The blinds were drawn and the semidark room, with dozens of plants by a patio door and more plants crowding the tables, made Marti think of a forest. Among the plants, a parrot gazed at her from a brass cage suspended from the ceiling. The parrot said "Son of Jaws" and looked away.

"What did you want to see me about?" Marti asked.

"DaVon's dead."

"I know."

"Cantor's dead, Johnny's dead . . . "

"Johnny's been dead a long time," Marti reminded her.

Leotha stared at her for a minute. "How much did they tell you about that?" she asked.

"Damned little, I suspect," Marti said. If Leotha knew more, she had never let on.

"Vice Deputy Riordan was our lieutenant then."

Marti nodded. "And Lieutenant Murphy was Johnny's sergeant." Dan Crosby, now retired, had been vice deputy then, and Riordan, Crosby's protégé. Interesting, the way the boys from Bridgeport kept things in the family.

"Crosby was insisting that cocaine hadn't arrived in Chicago," Leotha said. "He ordered all the narc units to work quick street busts, no long-term investigations."

Marti remembered Johnny coming home filled with frustration because Crosby had told one of the newspapers that the drug problem in Chicago was under control and certainly much less severe than the problem in Detroit, or L.A. or New York. "He's never walked a beat," Johnny had said. "He doesn't know what in the hell is out there. The death rate for crack users is climbing every month and he still insists that our biggest problem is heroin. Man's got his head in his . . . "

Leotha lit another cigarette from the butt of the last. "Johnny had spent weeks setting up a major crack buy. It was going down the night he died."

Marti was surprised to hear something that big was going on.

"Riordan was going to prove that we had a major cocaine problem. Word was that Riordan even had a reporter on standby so they couldn't cover it up. It was going down at eight-thirty. In time for the ten o'clock news. Riordan had two of his teams on it, twenty of us."

Marti felt a tightness in her chest. There was no way Johnny would have let the dealer change the time or done anything else that could have caused things to go wrong. Johnny must have been going to see a snitch then, like DaVon said—but why, with something that big about to go down? DaVon had lied to her when he said it was a routine bust. Why? What else had he lied about?

"DaVon said it was a routine buy."

"It's not something any of us talk about. This one was big. Riordan told us it was a dead bang," Leotha said. "A sure thing. Johnny was his sure thing. When Johnny went way undercover like that, he'd sit maybe two, three hours before the deal went down, and say nothing, absolutely nothing. By the time he went in, I think he was totally inside their heads. And he always came out."

Seeing a snitch would have broken his concentration. He wouldn't have done that. But that's what DaVon said. What had really happened that night? With DaVon dead, would she ever know?

"Riordan was furious when Johnny went down and the buy never came off. We made the small-time busts because that was Crosby's directive, but Riordan was always after something big.

"Until that bust was set up, Riordan would put Johnny and a couple other guys on something long-term, falsify the records so it looked like they were in on the small stuff. Then, when something big went down, he'd make like his guys stumbled onto it. Johnny didn't often get credit for the bust, to keep Crosby from suspecting that the bigger busts Johnny always set up weren't coincidental."

Johnny had been doing this routinely and Marti had no idea. She believed he was just making street buys. He never told her. Why? "What happened that night that they didn't tell me?"

"I wish I knew. None of it makes sense. Johnny didn't . . . you'd have to see him get up for something like that. He was just totally focused. There's no way he'd jeopardize a major bust. I don't know. It didn't make sense then, it doesn't now. DaVon said he was meeting a snitch, but if he was, it would have to have been something really big. Johnny never did anything to disrupt his focus. He didn't even eat before a big bust, except for M&M's."

Johnny never told Marti any of this. As soon as he joined the Narcotics Unit, everything he did became top secret.

"Why are you telling me this now, Leotha, because your ass is on the line with Riordan? There's nothing I can do about that. Cantor's death didn't have anything to do with Johnny's."

Johnny's death was not going to become some kind of pawn for Rachel Cantor or Leotha. If only someone did know how he died, or why. The way things were now, anyone could come along and insinuate whatever they wanted. A dull throbbing began at her temples.

Leotha scanned the newspaper. "You read this yet? You see what they got last night? Thirty-two kilos, quarter of a million dollars, major suburban dealer. The kind of bust Riordan lives for. It saved Murphy's ass and he probably knew less about what was going on than the dealers did. And DaVon is a hero."

"Not like when Cantor went down," Marti reminded her. "You're being investigated because of that."

Leotha blew smoke in her direction. "Cantor was way under. He had this damned street persona that he could put on and wear like a hat. He was the 'Nam vet, a little burned-out, a little crazy. He swore to God he was a drug runner during the war. He really knew the language. Suckered them right in. Made major buys with as much effort as a junkie scoring dime bags. We had a meeting four days before he went down. He asked a lot of questions about the night Johnny died."

"Like what?"

"Who he was with that day, who he called, who he saw, where he went. If anything unusual had happened that week."

"What did you tell him?"

"Not a hell of a lot. I only saw Johnny for a few minutes that day. He was real quiet all that week, same as he always was when something major was going down."

"Did you tell Murphy and Riordan that his behavior wasn't unusual?"

"When they got around to asking me, yes. But by then, everything was official."

"What else did Cantor want to know?"

"He wanted to know how everyone reacted after it happened. And what I really knew about what went down."

"What do you know?"

"Exactly what they told you. DaVon found him. Homicide sealed off that whole area fast. DaVon couldn't go back in. Murphy and Riordan couldn't. Nobody got in there, except Crosby. None of us were told anything. We got the same information you did."

"Did you believe it?"

Leotha looked at her for a moment. "Did you?"

Marti shook her head. "But he was found in a cemetery, alone. There was no evidence that anyone was with him." And Johnny had been quiet that week, more so than usual. And, as she was finding out now, there was an awful lot going on that he never told her about. There could have been something else, something she still didn't know. She could not believe it was suicide. She did know him better than that.

Leotha lit another cigarette. "Everything on Johnny's case is restricted. There is no information available. Nothing. I can't get access, but you're family, you can."

Why were the records sealed? Instead of wondering aloud and allowing Leotha to become aware of how little she knew, Marti asked, "Was DaVon where he said he was that night?"

She hated asking that question. Partners did everything but go to the bathroom together. But DaVon had lied to her.

"I assume so. That was never questioned as far as I know. Cantor asked about that, too."

"Why was he asking so many questions?"

"He promised we'd talk about that in a few days."

"What happened to him?"

"How do I know? When you work for an asshole like Murphy, a lot of things can happen."

Johnny thought Murphy had reached his level of incompetence as a sergeant and predicted advancement. "Man's never made a decision in his life," Johnny said. "Comes to work wearing a brown suit with a gray tie. Closes his eyes and reaches into the closet."

A thin layer of smoke floated above Leotha's head. "I tell my men over and over, stick with the plan, stick with the plan. Trouble is, you ask Murphy what the plan is, and he says he'll get back to you. So I come up with a plan, the other sergeants come up with a plan. We're all doing our own thing, trying to keep our units in sync . . . "

"Who's Murphy's chinaman?" Marti asked.

"I'm not sure. I thought it must be Riordan, but now I don't think so."

"Crosby was vice deputy chief of narcotics when Johnny died. Maybe it's him."

"No. As soon as it was impossible for Crosby to deny that the dealers who had been into heroin for years were doing big business in cocaine, he took early retirement. The department was not prepared for a crack epidemic, thanks to him. How much clout can he have?"

"You think Cantor fell over that ledge?"

"I don't know what he was doing on that roof. If he wasn't dead, I'd kill him. And if his partner's doing any talking, he sure ain't talking to me. The buy never went down, and I needed it, big time. We've all got our agendas. Riordan wants to beef up his statistics so we're doing a lot of small busts. He wants fame, so we have to give him big busts, too. Murphy wants to hide in his office and let everyone else make his decisions. I want to make one or two dealers at least wonder if they're in charge of the streets or we are, and maybe keep one shipment out of the projects or the school yard. Bottom line, we've got all these cowboys making field decisions, dropping fifty thousand dollars on a bad bust and getting killed to boot."

Fifty thousand. "The department's not laying out that kind of money."

"Of course not. The DEA is. It's small change to them. We tie into some DEA action, take out a few of the big boys. Cantor worked with them a lot. I couldn't waste him on the petty shit . . . "

Listening to Leotha made Marti realize how hard she had worked to keep a low profile and stay out of the politics when she worked here. She was glad to be out of it, glad she was in Lincoln Prairie.

"Look, Leotha, I'm not sure I want to know all of this. I'm sorry about what happened to Cantor, I'm sorry they're trying to make you take a fall, but I don't see what any of it has to do with me, or with Johnny."

Leotha looked at her with a brooding expression. "You're not listening, MacAlister. You don't want to hear me. Cantor's partner was in the parking garage, one level below. The deal went down early. The exchange was made—they found the drugs on Cantor, which means they wanted him and they didn't give a damn about giving up the shit to get him. The question is, why did he go over? Someone had to know he was a cop. Why didn't they get his partner, too? They know we travel in pairs.

"And why did they take DaVon out, because he was the first man in? Do you know how happy they are to see us when we holler 'police'? How grateful they are that we're not another dealer? Other dealers kill them, kill their families, their babies. They're glad when it's us. They get to make bail, stay alive, sell more shit."

"I'm still not with you," Marti said.

"First Johnny goes down, then Cantor asks questions about Johnny and Cantor goes down. Then DaVon, the one person who

could know something about Johnny's death that he's not telling, goes down."

"Sorry, Leotha, based on the little that I do know, I don't see how what happened to Johnny three years ago could have any impact on what's happening now. I think this is all just coincidence," Marti said. "I don't know what happened to Johnny that night. I don't know why he went to that cemetery. I don't know if DaVon told the truth. And I don't believe that Johnny ate his gun, but as much as I need to find out the truth, you have nothing that makes any of this hang together."

Marti phoned home to say she'd be late for dinner, then arranged to meet Vik at the Barrister.

"You know the narc who got killed last night, too?" Vik asked, grabbing a handful of pretzels.

"DaVon Holmes." Marti had a sudden clear impression of DaVon. Not the man swaddled in coat, muffler, and hat the other night, but the man who rode with Johnny. The man with the loud, boisterous laugh that made her want to laugh, too. The man who told great jokes with perfect timing. The man who could put his sense of humor on hold when Johnny needed to be quiet, or become a stand-up comedian when Johnny was taking things too seriously and needed to laugh. "He was Johnny's partner."

In Polish, Vik said, *"No i coz."*

"What now? Or what about it?" she asked, not sure which he meant.

"Both."

"Let's take tomorrow afternoon off and go into the city. I want to see Commander Rivas, he's in charge of Internal Affairs."

Vik whistled. "How come?"

"Just for the hell of it, and because IA has restricted all of the records pertaining to Johnny's death. It's as good a place to start as any, and I think we want them to know we're asking questions."

"Is Holmes's death an 'accident,' too?"

"No. Line of duty. The only thing I can think of that's more

dangerous than manning a ram is working on a bomb squad or making traffic stops."

"What do you think happened?"

"The odds caught up with him. Johnny liked to work undercover. DaVon liked to break down doors. Risky, all of it, but DaVon always laid his life on the line."

"And Johnny?"

"With Johnny, it was easy to make a case for suicide. Cops do eat their guns. DaVon told them Johnny was there to meet with a snitch, but there wasn't any evidence to support it. Besides, Leotha told me what was really going on. Whatever happened with Johnny, they had other things they had to cover up. I don't know . . . " Her voice shook.

She clenched a fist and stared at a water spot on the ceiling until she felt calmer. "I don't know what was more important to them, investigating Johnny's death or covering up what was going on. I think they tried the same thing with Rachel that they pulled on me—pushed a few buttons and suicide worked. I knew they couldn't prove what happened and that I couldn't disprove whatever they said happened. Johnny was a good cop. I didn't want anyone to take that away from him. Accidental was an easy way out. I took it. I know more now than I did then." Things Johnny should have told her. Things she needed to know when he died.

Vik was incredulous as she explained about the long-term investigations.

"They weren't authorized to do that?"

"No. They were supposed to make street buys and busts."

"And there wasn't any cocaine out there?"

"Not officially, just heroin."

"Subversive activity within the department." Vik shook his head. "They just ignored orders and did as they pleased?"

"They wanted to get to the dealers. Johnny's lieutenant, who is now the vice deputy by the way, didn't want his boss to know what was going on. When they made a major bust, they said they had walked into something. Johnny worked the long-term investigations, but his name probably doesn't show up on the reports of

all of the busts he was in on. Crosby, who was vice deputy then, would have caught on."

"And Johnny was on one of these investigations when he died, so they covered up the whole thing?"

"I think so."

"How did Johnny feel about falsifying reports?"

Johnny never told her. "Once he started working Narcotics, he never brought the job home." Not verbally. His silence should have told her something. She thought he felt the way she did about homicide, like leaving it "out there" when she came home.

"It's hard to imagine a lieutenant running that kind of an operation against department policy. No wonder you're mad."

"I'm not." She saw Vik watching as she unclenched her fist. "So maybe I am. What good does it do now?"

10

Joanna was in the kitchen preparing a chicken and shrimp stir-fry for supper when Marti got home. As Marti watched, Joanna chopped bok choy until it looked like confetti, then minced the jicama. When she reached for the carrots, Marti said, "Aren't the pieces supposed to be bigger than that?"

Joanna kept at it until the carrots were chopped finely enough to make cole slaw.

When Marti reached out to her, Joanna moved away. Tears glistened in her eyes.

"What's wrong?"

"Why would anything be wrong?"

Joanna hadn't seemed upset when they talked about DaVon this morning. Maybe she had an argument with her boyfriend.

"Is it Chris?"

"No. Why would it be him?"

"Well, since it's not DaVon . . . "

"Is that where you were? At the funeral home?"

It was DaVon. "No. They haven't . . . " She stopped without saying they wouldn't have released the body yet. "I thought you didn't remember him."

"Well, I didn't want to, but he came to the house after Daddy died." She wiped at her eyes. "He said Daddy was the best partner he ever had. He said he would miss him, just like we would. He told me that he was sorry he wasn't there when Daddy needed him."

Marti knew DaVon had been to the house, either before or after the funeral, but she didn't even have an impression of whether he

was in uniform, let alone recall anything that he said. She was angry with him then.

"I'm sorry. I didn't know."

Joanna sniffled and blew her nose. "It's okay. He just seemed like a really nice man. Oh, ma." Joanna hugged her. "I know it's safer here, being a cop, for you anyway. But . . . "

"I know. Sometimes you worry. Sometimes you're scared. I'm sorry."

"I just don't want anything to happen to you."

Marti hugged her. "Me neither." Then she thought of Theo. "Did DaVon talk to your brother, too?"

"Yes, but Theo doesn't remember."

"Is he okay?" He had seemed all right this morning, quiet, but all right.

"Who's okay in this house when a cop gets shot, ma? Officer Holmes's picture was on the news. Maybe Theo recognized him. He didn't say."

Marti found Theo down in the family room working on the computer. She pulled up a chair.

"What are you doing?"

"I'm making a file on the Potawatomi. This is a timeline."

"How's it going, Theo?"

"You mean about Daddy's partner getting killed?"

"Yes." Marti moved a little closer, surprised that he was talking about it so easily.

"I don't remember him." Theo kept typing as he spoke. "They shot the man who killed him and arrested everyone else. That's good."

"Theo . . . "

He reached for a book he had bought at the museum. "Look at this, ma. There's lots of neat stuff in here about the Potawatomi."

Marti looked at the pictures as he pointed them out. He had said a lot more than she expected. That might mean that he was more upset than he seemed to be. She sat with him until Joanna called them to dinner. Twice she mentioned DaVon, twice Theo talked about something else.

Ben and Mike were taking off their coats when Marti went

upstairs. As a paramedic with the fire department, Ben worked two days on and one day off. Mike would stay with them tonight and tomorrow night. Marti frequently worried that the boys were having morbid conversations about deceased parents, but tonight she was glad that Theo would have company.

As Joanna served the stir-fry over noodles, Ben caught Marti's eye and raised his eyebrows.

Marti mouthed the word "Later" when Joanna wasn't looking.

After supper they all played Scrabble until it was time for the boys to go to bed. Joanna and Lisa went upstairs to do homework. Sharon excused herself with, "Alone at last, you two. I suppose you'll just talk." She had told Marti she was getting over one of her celibate phases, and tonight she was headed for either "a movie or a motel, depending." Marti and Ben were settling on the sofa to listen to the stereo when a car horn honked and Sharon ran out.

"Does she always do that?" Ben asked.

"I don't think she wants me to meet them. And since I've lived here, nobody she's dated has lasted long enough to make an introduction important. Frank's second wife is about to have a baby and she's been angry about that ever since she found out." Marti tried not to worry. "She doesn't pick these guys up in bars, she meets them through friends or at church. This one is probably just a distraction."

"Carol and I knew Sharon when she was still married to Frank."

Ben had only recently begun talking about his first wife.

"Did you see much of them?" Marti asked.

"We went to some of the same places. The Elks Club, Urban League and NAACP fundraisers, things like that. Frank wasn't . . . friendly."

"You noticed that," Marti agreed. Johnny's description of Frank was "donkey," a word he used when he didn't want to say ass. "I never did figure out why she married him. Opposites, Johnny used to say. We grew up together, but I went to U of I Chicago. Sharon was into afros and dashikis and wanted to go to a black college, so she went to Spelman. Frank went to Morehouse. That's where they met. Lord knows why she didn't leave him there, all the trouble he's caused her."

"Well, he moved without leaving any friends behind." Smiling, he put his arm about her shoulders. "I'm sure glad Sharon decided to stay."

Marti rested her head against his chest, catching a whiff of his aftershave. They sat like that for a while. "So, what were you chasing after in Chicago today?" Ben said. "Has it got anything to do with that cop who went down last night?"

"DaVon was Johnny's partner," Marti said. She began filling him in on her visit with Leotha until Joanna came in and interrupted.

"Theo had a nightmare."

Theo was awake but drowsy when Marti went upstairs. His dreams hadn't disturbed Mike, who was sound asleep in the top bunk, or Bigfoot, who looked up at Marti and dozed off again. She brought Theo warm milk laced with honey and vanilla, Momma's recipe for chasing away bad dreams.

"You feel better?"

He nodded and sipped from the mug. When he finished she said, "Let's cuddle." He snuggled beside her. "Want to talk?"

Theo shook his head. He never told her the dreams that awakened him. There hadn't been any in a while.

"Is this because of DaVon? Is that making you remember something about your dad?"

"No, ma. It was just a dream, and I wasn't dreaming about that cop who died."

He said it so quickly that Marti guessed he was lying. She pulled him against her. "Your dad did a very dangerous job. DaVon, too. They were very brave, both of them."

"Are you brave?"

"No. Not as brave as they were. My job is much safer." That wasn't exactly a lie.

"Good." He snuggled closer.

"This is a rough time of year for us. And I think maybe you might be a little upset with your dad for not being here for Webelos. That's okay. Sometimes I get a little upset with him for not being here, too."

She held him until his breath came slow and even. Then she

eased his head onto the pillow and adjusted the blankets.

Downstairs, she returned to her niche on Ben's shoulder. It was nice to be held again.

"First Cantor, now Johnny's partner," Ben said. "This must be rough on you."

"I don't know." She told him about her visit with Leotha. "She says she believes Julian Cantor and DaVon Holmes's deaths are somehow connected to Johnny's, but her shield is on the line now that they've named her in the Cantor investigation. I'm not sure what she thinks I can do that might help her."

"Maybe just distract them. Get them off her case."

Marti explained about the investigations Johnny had been involved in.

"Sounds like stuff that happened in 'Nam."

"Really?" Then maybe it wasn't so difficult for Johnny to deal with. Johnny never talked about 'Nam either, except to say he never wanted to have any cats or dogs in the house, whatever that meant. He had made an exception for Bigfoot because Joanna begged him.

"I think I've gotten complacent working in Lincoln Prairie," Marti said. "I can distance myself from the politics and there isn't that constant overload—poverty, crime, filth. Some of the homicides even make sense, to the perpetrator anyway. At least the motives make more sense than getting out of your car on the wrong corner or going to the store at the wrong time of day."

She had never told Ben about her old job. With Johnny, sometimes when something slipped out he either distracted her or changed the subject.

"Ben," she said, "the last weekend that I worked in Chicago, I had to pick up some evidence at the morgue. They had eleven gunshot deaths during the night, over two hundred bodies in the cooler, and as I was walking by, someone opened the cooler door and I saw these boxes stacked up inside. Plain wooden boxes. And I asked how many. Thirty-two. They were unidentified bodies ready to be taken for burial. I hear the numbers when I listen to the news. I read about the most important homicides in the newspaper, but I forget how overwhelming it is."

Marti looked at him.

"Sounds like 'Nam," he said.

"One night I had a stabbing, a wino who died of natural causes, an arson with three victims, two of them children. When they brought them out, they were covered with soot. I wanted to throw up. I wanted to cry. But I couldn't. I would have been a female cop again if I did. Then, just before my watch was over, I got called out on a drive-by shooting. The victim was thirteen, had just graduated from elementary school. I don't know how I dealt with all of that."

"After a while, you get numb, and you went home to Johnny."

"Who was probably as bummed out by what he saw as I was." Were the streets overwhelming to him, too? He was always so wired when he came home. Sometimes it took hours to come down. But not those last few weeks. Maybe he was burned-out. How would she have known that?

"We didn't talk much about the specifics. Maybe we should have." It felt good, saying this out loud. "We danced a lot late at night, even when we were tired. We made this little world for ourselves, just us and the kids and my mother. And then he died, and everything came inside. Maybe we protected the kids too much. Maybe that's why Theo still has nightmares."

"Mike had one a couple of months ago," Ben said. "I don't think protecting them has anything to do with it."

"Mike still has nightmares, too?" Marti said. Why did she always think she and her kids were the only ones? "I'm glad you're here to tell me things like that."

"I know," Ben said. "I didn't have anyone to compare notes with either." He pulled her closer. "With all of this, and the kids getting upset, you must be exhausted."

11

At seven-thirty Monday morning, Marti and Vik were standing behind a fire department barricade fifty feet from the smouldering heap of brick that had been a bar called Mary's Place. So much for going to Chicago today, Marti thought. Whatever caused the explosion had all but leveled the building. The fire that followed had consumed everything but the brick. The building had stood alone, separated by vacant lots from a TV repair shop on one side and a barber shop on the other. There had been two apartments on the floor above the bar.

The odor of burned wood and melted plastic got stronger as the wind shifted and smoke blew in their direction. Icicles were forming where the hoses connected to the hydrants. Marti could see the firemen's breath as they called to each other. She shivered as a frigid wind blew in from the lake, just a few blocks away. Despite her scarf, hat, gloves, and boots, she was cold.

"Damned shame," Vik said. "I remember that place when it was the Home Run Inn."

"When was that?" Marti asked.

"Fifteen, twenty years ago."

"I suppose the owner was your father's brother's wife's second cousin."

Vik rubbed his hands together. He didn't have his gloves. "The guy who built the place went to school with my brother."

Marti hadn't met many members of Vik's family. She wondered how much he and his two brothers were alike. It was impossible to think of Vik as the baby of the family. She wondered if they did. "Neighbor to the right says the bartender usually got here about six and there were a few regulars in there by seven," she said.

"Two men lived alone in the upstairs apartments. One owns that blue Chevy. The other one's car is gone."

"Well, if any of them were in there, they got blown to bits. And with the fire, we'll be lucky to recover a few body parts." He grimaced. "Damned shame about the building. We used to go there for beer and pizza and watch the Cubs or the Bears. Now all that's left is the basement."

"Think it was a terrorist bombing?" Marti teased.

"This isn't Chicago," Vik said. "People here don't do things like that."

Marti scanned the crowd. Nine people across the street. Fourteen standing around her, and one either had a cold or was crying.

"I'll take the other side," Vik said. He had counted the number of people, too. "We'll need some idea of the possible body count when they get the place cooled down and can look around."

Marti identified the source of the sniffles. She searched through her purse until she found a couple of tissues that weren't too wrinkled. Smiling, she offered them to a woman who was about to wipe her nose on the sleeve of a brown coat that looked like something the Salvation Army would reject.

"Oh, thanks." The woman smiled. "You're a doll."

Marti resisted the impulse to say, No, I'm a cop. She was cold. She was tired and cranky because she hadn't slept well last night. But she was going to remain calm and pleasant. "Are you feeling all right, ma'am?"

"No, I'm not. I feel awful." The woman dabbed at her eyes, careful not to smear her blue eyeshadow. She was wearing red lipstick and had bright splotches of rouge rubbed on prominent cheekbones.

"Poor Ed," the woman said. "That poor, dear man." She fluttered the tissues in the direction of the building. "How dreadful. How absolutely . . . terrible. It's . . . gone. And Ed . . . my God."

"Are you a friend?" Marti asked, hoping the question wouldn't prompt more theatrics.

"Oh, that poor, dear man. Always thinking of others, never a care for himself. He put one of those little things right by the cash register where you could give your change to crippled children."

Marti nodded. "You knew him?"

"And his children. My God! His wife. That poor, dear woman."

"What's your name, ma'am?"

"Irene. Irene O'Connor."

"Miss O'Connor, could you please tell me who Ed is?"

"The bartender, of course. He opened up every morning at six-thirty. He hasn't opened late one time this entire winter, as bad as the weather has been."

"You're sure about that?"

"Of course. I'm here every day before seven."

"Every day?"

"I haven't missed in over a year. Where else would I find someone as reliable as Ed?" Tears welled in her eyes. "Now where will I go?"

"What time did you get here this morning, Miss O'Connor?"

"About six-forty. The fire engines were already here."

"Did you let anyone know that Ed might be in there?"

"Why would I?" She seemed puzzled. "There wasn't any building anymore, so there wasn't any Ed, either."

"Anybody live upstairs?"

"A couple of sailors, I think. I ain't never seen them."

"You see any other customers hanging around when you got here?"

"Nah. Smitty and Gordy don't show up 'til about seven." Turning, she pointed to a man across the street. "That's Gordy. Antisocial. Never has so much as a good morning for the rest of us. Chug-a-lugs two double scotches and nurses draft beer until eight, then goes to work. He's a mailman."

Marti caught Vik's attention and pointed to Gordy. "Every day?" she asked.

"Yup. Same as me. I see Gordy here every day and he ain't never got nothing to say, no Merry Christmas, no Happy Thanksgiving, no nothing. Just like I said, antisocial."

"Is Smitty here, too?"

The woman took another look around. "Nah. He's found another bar. He'd be having the DTs by now if he hung around. It's

me and Gordy who won't have no place to go."

"There are other bars."

"This wasn't a bar." Tears spilled over and made streaks in her rouge. "This wasn't just a bar, not to me."

When Marti spoke with the head of the bomb and arson team, he was certain that the explosion was caused by a natural gas leak.

"What? No terrorist bombs?" Vik said.

"Bombs? Come on, Jessenovik, you been hanging with a Chicago cop too long."

Vik came very close to smiling.

By noon the bartender was still missing but Marti and Vik had located the sailors who rented the upstairs apartments. Irene O'Connor returned a little before one. The crowd had shrunk to seven diehards, probably hoping to see a few body bags as they watched the firemen poke through the debris.

Irene grabbed Marti by the arm and pointed to a man sitting on the curb across the street. "There's Smitty."

That lowered the count to one person believed to be inside at the time of the explosion—Ed, that poor, dear man.

Irene clung to Marti's arm as they walked across the street. She swayed as she spoke. "Offzer, this is my frien', Smitty. He knew Ed, too, God rest his soul."

"Sure did, and we . . . " Smitty's voice trailed off and he stared in the direction of the lake.

"Smitty, doll, tell the offzer here what you know . . . "

Smitty looked at Irene as if it was the first time he'd ever seen her. "Huh? Wha' ya say?"

Marti suggested that they both go home and take a little nap, then went to tell the arson investigators to cross Smitty off the list of possible victims.

Poor, dear Ed showed up at two-thirty. He was short, pot bellied, with red hair, a bulbous nose and bowed legs.

"My God, this is unbelievable. I can't believe it." He walked across the street, as if he could get things in better perspective from that distance, then returned, shaking his head. "I can't believe it."

"You didn't open up this morning?" Marti said.

"No. I had a doctor's appointment in Evanston. Just a little prostate trouble. Not cancer, thank God."

He turned away, walked to the curb, came back again. "I can't believe this."

"Why didn't you tell anyone where you were going?"

"I put a sign on the door. Oh, my God. You mean, you thought . . . " He threw up his hands. "I can't believe it."

It was a little after six when Marti and Vik were called back to the scene of the explosion. Skeletal remains had been found beneath the foundation. Old bones, according to Coroner Janet Petroski, bones undamaged by the explosion and fire.

12

Marti was alone in the kitchen late Monday night, sitting in the rocking chair with the lamp on, when Rachel Cantor called. Marti had been reading the *Chicago Tribune,* careful to avoid the article about DaVon in the lower right corner of page three.

"They brought Julian's things home today," Rachel said.

Julian's partner must have cleaned out his locker. Anything he didn't think Rachel should see would have been tossed out. Rachel would have everything else as well as any personal effects the investigating officers didn't need as evidence.

Johnny hadn't kept much in his locker. DaVon had come to the house with a plastic shopping bag. A few hours after DaVon left, she'd looked inside.

Marti felt a sharp pain in her wrist and loosened her grip on the receiver. "How are you?"

"They put everything in a box that was used to pack grapefruit. Julian hated them. I have a trunk with his army uniforms. Maybe I'll put them there."

Marti had packed Johnny's things in a suitcase that she kept on a shelf in her closet.

"They kept his notebook," Rachel said, "but there are other notes that they don't know about. You know how they are about their notebooks. And I know your notebooks can be used as evidence in court. For Julian working without one was like going out without his clothes on. They must teach you that at the academy. Never, never leave home without it."

"That's true." Using a notebook was so ingrained that Marti couldn't imagine ever being without one.

When Johnny was undercover, he said he felt as uneasy without his notebook as he did without his shield. They all had a code word that changed each day so they could identify themselves to another cop if they had to, but not having any identification or his notebook always bothered him.

"Julian rolled cigarettes," Rachel said. "He didn't smoke them, he wrote notes in Hebrew on the paper. I found two of them in the hem of his jacket, but I don't understand what they mean. I thought maybe Johnny did something like that, too, that what Julian wrote might mean something to you."

"What did he write?"

Rachel said something in Hebrew. "That's the word he used for informant. Then there's the word *Lope*. He used numbers for that instead of letters."

"Johnny used a deck of cards. I know the code, but someone had gone through the deck before they gave it to me."

"Then this doesn't mean anything to you?" Rachel sounded disappointed. "I thought maybe it had something to do with Johnny."

Marti didn't say anything. She had gone through Johnny's cards again and again, trying to find something that might begin to explain why he had died. Maybe it was just as well someone had disturbed the order of the deck. She had no words like *Lope* to recall again and again, to puzzle over and become frustrated by when she couldn't figure out their meaning. Marti wanted to tell Rachel to throw the cigarettes away, to let go, but they were such a tangible link to Julian. There were others—a song, a place, an odor—that odd, jarring recollection that seemed to come without provocation. Like Momma said, memories just sneak up and grab hold of you.

Upstairs, Marti went to the closet and took down the small suitcase, placing it on her bed. As she opened it, the smell of perspiration, though faint, seemed overwhelming. She always called that Johnny's "good-bye aroma," even though he didn't smell that way until he came home. He always complained because unscented deodorant didn't hold up. She always wondered what it was about the job that caused him to perspire so heavily.

They had returned a shirt and jacket and his bulletproof vest because he wasn't wearing them when he died, but kept the rest of his clothing. She wasn't home when he left the house, and it was only after she packed everything that was going to Am Vets that she realized he had been wearing a faded green-striped shirt he usually put on when he did yard work.

Marti touched Johnny's leather shoulder holster. He hadn't been wearing that either. His wallet—not the one that held his buy money, the one that would have been in his locker—had forty dollars and a few credit cards, one family photograph and snapshots of her and the kids. She didn't look at them tonight. Maybe she should give his watch to Theo now. Or should she wait? Until when?

Johnny did talk to her, mostly late at night and when they were alone, but he talked. Not about the job or what he did that day, never about anything that happened in 'Nam, but he talked about things that happened when they were growing up, or what they might do when they retired, or about what was going on with Theo and Joanna. They did talk. They had even begun talking about having another child.

Johnny must have talked with Theo, too, when they were working on Scout projects together or mowing the grass or running errands. Did Theo remember that? Or did he just recall the quiet, somber Johnny who listened to music wearing earphones, pantomiming a sax player or tapping on an imaginary drum?

Theo wasn't as quiet then. He laughed more, and sometimes, like Johnny, made cryptic one-word comments that she could decipher. He didn't do that anymore. Maybe she needed to know what Theo remembered, remind him of a man he couldn't quite recall. She would talk with him more, like last night.

Marti took the tattered blue and white box out of the suitcase, took out the playing cards, worn at the edges. Looking close, she could see where Johnny's daddy, a gambling man, had marked them. They were sweat stained in places where they had once been white, with some of the red on the diamonds and hearts and the black on the clubs and spades rubbed away. They felt soft, almost warm, in her hands.

She knew Johnny's code. Each numeric heart, diamond, and club represented a letter of the alphabet. The deuce of spades was the letter A and the trey was Z. The other spades meant trouble of some kind, or caution, depending on what was spelled out; liar or lying, unreliable, weapon, violent, danger. The red aces and the king, queen, and jack of hearts were vowels. The other royals were words such as arrest, record, witness, drugs, dealer, informant, but if they were used with a numeric card, that meant the card was a number.

When Marti opened the deck after Johnny died, she expected him to talk to her through the symbols, but he did not. When she wrote out the code based on the way the cards were arranged, it was meaningless. She went through the deck until she could no longer deny that the cards did not hold any secrets. There was not even a good-bye message. Johnny would not have willingly left her without somehow saying good-bye. Someone must have flipped through them, destroying the order.

Now, as she lined up the cards on the quilted bedspread, she saw the same jumble again. DaVon had said Johnny was meeting an informant. The jack of clubs—informant—did not follow a name, and the letters preceding it were initials, which Johnny didn't often use. They meant nothing to Marti.

Or did they? Marti got a pencil and piece of paper. Without disturbing the order again she flipped over each card as she had done three years before and spelled out the letters and numbers that were there. Then she picked up the cards, stroking the blue and white backs, remembering them in Johnny's strong, dark hands, being caressed by his long, slender fingers. Thinking back even further, she remembered Johnny's father, his dark face stern and inscrutable, a toothpick dangling from the corner of his mouth as he dealt them. She could remember him coming to the hospital with Johnny when Theo was born, refusing to use a cane but aware that his next stroke could be his last. He stood with his face near the nursery window, tears coursing down his cheeks, and looked at his namesake. Despite the sternness and the silence, there was love between those two men, and they had shared that love with Theo. Did Theo remember? Could not knowing for certain how his father died overshadow everything else?

Marti returned everything to the suitcase. She looked at the letters and numbers on the sheet of paper for a long time. There was nothing that could be even loosely interpreted as snitch, and no two letters in the word *Lope* were sequential. Those words were part of Julian's secrets. What if they were part of Johnny's secrets, too? If Julian really had been asking about Johnny . . . If Julian really had heard Johnny's name, had the messages in Julian's code once been part of another code, one that was permanently obliterated?

She stared at the page of deciphered code until it blurred. Tears were hot on her face as she crushed the paper. She sat on the edge of the bed with her hands clenched and took deep breaths. This jumbled message from the cards was all the good-bye she would ever have. She smoothed out the paper and put it in the nightstand drawer.

13

I t was a little before five when Marti woke up Tuesday morning. The first thing she thought of was "snitch" and *Lope*. She knew Johnny was seeing a snitch—maybe that was why it seemed like such a trivial thing to hide in such an elaborate way. *Lope* meant nothing. Maybe neither meant anything, as far as Johnny's death was concerned. The frustration was in not knowing.

Marti reached for the phone. "Sorry if I woke you," she said when Leotha answered.

"No problem. Wait'll I get a cigarette." A moment later Leotha said, "What's up?"

"Maybe nothing. I just wanted to ask you a few questions."

"Does that mean you're ready to pursue this, MacAlister?"

"It means I think it's time I made a few inquiries about Johnny."

"Good. That'll take you right to Cantor and DaVon."

"Maybe. But I don't know what I'll find out. If you help me, there might not be any payoff for you at all."

"So?"

"Were Cantor and DaVon friends?"

"Acquaintances. Most of DaVon's off-duty friends were women. And DaVon was working short-term investigations, and Cantor long-term."

"Is there any way they could have run into each other recently?"

Leotha thought for a minute. "In the past month we've had a wake for Jerry Kraft, the instructor at the Academy who keeled over during class. A real Irish wake, lots of liquor. DaVon passed out in the bathroom, everyone left without him, and the undertaker found him wandering through the viewing rooms talking to the corpses about two in the morning. Then there was Sully's retirement party. DaVon got shit-faced again. Your best bet is the wake. A lot of us were sorry to see Jerry go. Cantor could have slipped in late to pay his respects."

Marti could remember DaVon's womanizing. But he didn't drink like that when he rode with Johnny. "Suppose there is more to all of this, Leotha? Do you really want to get involved?"

"You mean do I want to play it safe? Come out of this investigation with my star?" Leotha said. "Marti, I'm pushing fifty—hard. I'm black—no, African-American—and I'm female. That puts me in three protected categories according to the labor department and doesn't mean shit anywhere else.

"I've always played it safe, done whatever was politically correct, said purple when I knew damned good and well the sky was blue, held my liquor, covered my ass. I laughed at their stupid jokes, put up with their sexist behavior and ignored their racist remarks. And how do Murphy and Riordan repay me? You got it. They start playing grab-ass with my star. I work twice as hard, take three times as much shit and they still don't want me to have rank. I hope they are both into something up to their armpits and we find out what it is."

Marti didn't intend to get caught up in Leotha's vendetta, if there was one. But she might need Leotha's help.

"There is one other thing. I'd like to talk with Cantor's partner."

"He's under investigation, too. I'll ask him, but he doesn't even want to talk with me, right now. I think he has a lawyer."

"Do I know him?"

Leotha told her who he was, but the name wasn't familiar. "Who did DaVon ride with?"

"Jim Bauer."

Marti remembered him.

"He's on leave, went to his parents' place in the Upper Peninsula. He's talking about leaving the department."

"Great. Thanks for the info, and I'll keep in touch," Marti promised.

Next, she called Steve Yablonski, her partner when she left the department in Chicago.

"I need a favor, Ski."

"You got it."

"Thanks. I'm looking for a snitch. Someone DaVon Holmes might have seen or intended to see maybe three or four weeks ago. I'm not sure of the time frame. Maybe someone who wasn't a regular snitch or wasn't involved with narcotics. I don't know who's working the case, but . . . "

"Don't worry, kid. You got it."

When Marti arrived at the precinct, Dirkowitz wanted to see her and Vik right after roll call.

"What have you got on the remains found at the site of that explosion yesterday?" Dirkowitz asked, pacing from his desk to the window with his hands clasped behind his back. He never called them in to discuss a case this early in the investigation unless he was getting some flack.

"Everything is being hand-delivered to the Robert Stein Facility in Chicago this morning," Vik said, "but it'll be at least two weeks before we know anything."

"We're going through our open files, Sir," Marti said. "Checking out missing persons, going through the *News-Times* archives to see if there's anything on file that could be relevant."

"Good." The lieutenant ran his fingers through his blond hair. Thick-necked and broad shouldered, he still had the build of a linebacker. "Remember when that place was the Home Run Inn, Jessenovik?"

"I used to watch the Cubs games there with my old man."

"Well, a lot of other people seem to remember it from back then, too. Most of them called me yesterday, last night, or this morning."

"Anybody got an idea of who we might have found in there, Sir?" Vik asked.

"I'm glad you mentioned that." He handed Vik half a dozen pages from a legal pad, with three columns penciled in on each one. "You probably know some of the names. Quite a few sounded like old-timers. I've listed the caller, the phone number, and their best guess as to who we've found. A few thought they knew who might have done it as well as motive, method, and opportunity. I've noted that, too."

Vik's eyebrows almost met as he studied the list. "Nothing like having a lot of leads." He gnawed on the corner of his lower lip. He was not pleased.

The lieutenant seemed to be considering something as he looked out the window. He had a partial view of Lake Michigan, and the water was dark gray today.

"I have also had a call from a member of the local chapter of the NAACP, wondering if these might be the remains of an African-American who died during a journey along the underground railroad. This gentleman also called the mayor and several aldermen who have, in turn, called me."

"You do look a little tired, Sir," Vik said.

The lieutenant yawned and sat down. He picked up the baseball-shaped hand grenade that he kept on his desk, a reminder of a brother who died in Vietnam.

"A Native American has called to ask if we were pursuing the possibility that this was the site of a sacred burial ground. A member of the Committee to Create a National Casimir Pulaski Day has inquired into the ethnic origins of the remains. The Lincoln Prairie Historic Society is wondering if they have any local significance. And Salvatore Quintana's ex-wife called. It seems that Salvatore was presumed dead in a swimming mishap fifteen years ago, but since we have these old bones and they were found so close to the lake, maybe he met with foul play instead."

"We'll get this resolved as quickly as possible, Sir," Vik said. "But we will need the forensics to confirm identification. And that means . . . "

"I know, Jessenovik. There could be a considerable delay. Do what you can. I'll keep you apprised of the phone calls. The mayor has called a press conference at noon. And you will each comment on this investigation. I expect you to be brief, concise, and politically correct." Dirkowitz dropped the grenade on his desk, signalling the end of the meeting.

It didn't seem like a good time for Marti to mention anything about looking into Johnny's death. And although she would be able to take time off unless something else came up, with all the attention the skeletal remains were getting, they would have to put some time in on it while they were waiting for the forensic reports.

In the hallway, Marti turned to Vik. "We'll each take half of this list and get on the phone with these people and do a little PR work."

"And don't chit-chat," Vik said. "Shouldn't take more than a couple of hours. After the press conference, we're out of here."

By ten o'clock Marti and Vik were convinced that nobody on the lieutenant's list knew anything.

"Well-intentioned crackpots," Vik said. "And nuisance pains-in-the-butt. I've talked to at least half a dozen old biddies who think their neighbors have offed a relative. They'd need a telescope to observe most of what they say they've seen, and I bet they've got them."

Marti hadn't come up with any leads, either. It was a waste of time, but as eager as she thought she was to go to IA, the delay had given her a little more time to think about what Leotha had already told her. There was so much about Johnny's narc activities that she didn't know, she'd better be prepared for more surprises.

"The previous owners of the bar are in Boca Raton," Vik said.

"Maybe if the lieutenant's phone keeps ringing off the hook he'll send us down there to talk with them."

"Right, MacAlister, and maybe we won't get any more snow, and tulips will be coming up in the morning. We'll have to talk with the bartender and the three looneytunes who opened the place up every morning, those two servicemen. No rush. This one's been dead too long for any of them to have known who it was."

Slim, one of two vice cops who shared their office, sauntered in.

"You've got to stop showering in perfume every morning," Marti said.

Slim gave her a cupid's-bow smile. "Cologne."

"More like sewer water," she said. "You're destroying my sinuses."

"I love it when you talk dirty."

Slim's partner, Cowboy, came in with the coffee pot. "Court in half an hour," he drawled. "Slim, you ain't got time to hit on Marti this morning. This is the best case we've had in a month."

"Don't tell me," Vik said. "You caught the old guy who's been flashing at the nursing home."

"No, man, this is big," Slim said.

"Right," Cowboy agreed. "We caught a very well-known football player in flagrante delicto with one of our more popular little ladies of the night. She'll be celebrity hooker of the week when the *News-Times* hits the stands this afternoon."

"Today the *News-Times,* tomorrow *Playboy,*" Slim said.

"*Playboy?*" Cowboy said. "Chick looks like W. C. Fields in a nightgown."

"Well, maybe the lovely Lorinda sags a little bit here and there . . . "

"A little?" Cowboy said. "Damned disappointing, finding a man who can tackle like that in bed with someone like her. And at the Kon Tiki Motel. No class."

"Maybe one of the tabloids will pick it up," Slim said. "I wonder if they interview cops? Be a shame to waste space on a hooker and I've got a much better profile than our kinky corner back."

"Speaking of which," Cowboy said, "what's this I hear about our very own Dyspeptic Duo having a press conference today to discuss old bones?"

"A topic about which Jessenovik is vastly familiar," Slim said. "No offense Marti, but Cowboy is right, you and His Grumpiness have had a lot in common the past few days."

As she drove into Chicago, Marti and Vik discussed Johnny's long-term investigations.

"I still can't believe it," Vik said. "This Lieutenant Riordan ignores orders and does as he pleases. That's insubordination. And now he's in charge of the whole operation."

To Marti's surprise, Eduardo Rivas, who headed IA, had agreed to see them. Rivas was taller than Vik and thick-set. His neck seemed to merge with his shoulders, and he had a bald spot near the top of his head. Rivas was working at a computer when Marti and Vik went into his office. After he turned off the monitor, he came from behind his desk and shook hands with Marti and Vik.

"Please have a seat." He smiled, as if he had invited them. "How can I help you?"

"I'd like to see the files on my husband's death. I understand they're restricted."

"Yes, but not to his family. I'll get them." He spoke to his secretary, a male uniform.

Marti knew she had the right to see the files, but she hadn't expected it to be so easy. Why was Rivas being so cooperative?

"Now there are a few things we must discuss, MacAlister. First, the reports from the first two officers on the scene are missing."

"Missing? How could you allow anything to go missing? And don't bother telling me someone got careless."

"That's one of the reasons the file has been restricted. Also, there are several ongoing investigations that could be impacted by information contained here."

"The investigation Johnny was involved with when he died?" According to Leotha, that bust never went down.

"Among others, yes."

They would have to be major investigations if they were still pending after all this time. Marti didn't believe him.

"You may see this any time you'd like, make whatever notes you'd like, but I would appreciate it very much if you would not make any photocopies. In view of what has already happened, we need to have control of these records."

Marti said nothing.

"So," Rivas said. "You're in Lincoln Prairie now, and still working homicide?"

"Yes."

"And the children?"

"They're fine."

"This must have been a good move for them. More time with you after the loss of their father."

"Yes."

There was a knock and the young officer came in with the files.

Marti stared at the bulging expandable folder and the two envelopes labelled "photographs." Her stomach contracted until it felt like a fist. She thought it would take longer. She wasn't ready to see this.

Rivas stood up. "It's very good to see you looking so well. If I can be of any further assistance, don't hesitate to call. I'm on my way to a meeting, so if you'll come this way . . . " He showed them into a small conference room. A female officer joined them. She nodded and sat in a chair away from the table.

Vik sat across from Marti, taking everything out of the folder and placing it in a neat stack between them. Marti stared at the forms. What madness had brought her to this room? Johnny's name was on those forms. Descriptions of his death and dying were in the reports. The people who wrote them had looked at him until he became another body, another statistic, until he became the summation of details and circumstances that could be typed on pieces of paper. But he was so much more than that to her.

Marti took a deep breath. With steady hands, she picked up the first report and began to read, handing it to Vik when she was finished. It took a while, the process of detachment that allowed her to visualize the scene through the eyes of the technicians, but it came. Soon, she, too, was in the cemetery, feeling the chill of the almost spring air and smelling the sweet-rotting odor of the damp, dead leaves that had been trapped beneath winter snow. Soon she was following the evidence trail to the car parked near the tall yews.

When Marti came to the ballistics reports she remembered how Riordan and Crosby had thrown one question after another at her—questions she couldn't answer. How could someone have taken Johnny's gun away from him? How could anyone get that close to Johnny with a gun? Why were there powder burns on his hands? Her anger erupted so quickly that she seized the cup of coffee the secretary had brought in and was ready to throw it before she caught herself and put the cup down.

Was this why Rivas made it so easy for her to see these reports—so that once again she would become so upset that she wouldn't be able to get past the name of the weapon? She thought she was calm, rational, during those first hours and days and even weeks after Johnny died. Now she realized how distraught she had been, how desperately she had needed to block out the violence. Marti squeezed her eyes shut and took a deep breath. She picked up the first of the ballistics reports.

This time, she read the details of the bullet's destruction. Her vision blurred and her hand shook, but she kept reading, more certain than ever that Johnny would not have shot himself.

Next, Marti picked up the second version of the two officers' reports, written three days after they arrived at the scene, when the moment of discovery and someone else's interpretation of events could have merged. What was in the initial reports? These were worthless. She put them down.

Vik gestured toward the packets of photographs. Marti shook her head. Vik looked through them, without expression, careful to place each glossy side down. When he was ready to return them to the envelopes he looked at her again. Aware of the officer making herself inconspicuous, Marti mouthed the word "One."

Vik flipped through about a dozen before handing her one. Marti put the photograph on the table. It was a wide angle shot. The car was parked on a narrow road near a dense cluster of bushy yews. Brown leaves, thick as a carpet, covered the ground. The window on the driver's side was down. Johnny was sprawled across the seat, his left arm flung up obscuring his face. Marti wanted to gather him into her arms and rock him as she might a child. She wanted to stroke his hair and kiss his face and whisper "Be all right." She touched the picture with her fingertip, then handed the photograph to Vik.

As they walked to the parking lot, tiny flakes of icy snow started to fall. She gave Vik the car keys. They headed for the expressway, moving in fits and starts in the exodus from the Loop.

"Were there a lot of trees in the other pictures?" she asked.

"Yes."

"I waited on the other side near a mausoleum until they took him out . . . " She remembered weathered tombstones and a statue of a kneeling angel, but no trees. After 'Nam, Johnny wouldn't go

to Grant Park unless he had to. Why would he choose a place to kill himself where there were so many trees?

As they inched toward the on-ramp for the Kennedy, the words "ragged, starlike pattern," "tears and burn-ring around entrance wound," and "unburned carbon particles on skin" faded in Marti's mind and she saw him, sprawled on the seat. Alone. Alone. Alone. As Vik grumbled about "big city rush hour insanity," Marti put her hands to her face and cried.

14

Dan Riordan stood by the window, watching the traffic below. It was dark outside and he had turned off the light, something he often did when he wanted to think. Why, after all this time, was MacAlister's wife making inquiries? How much could she find out? How would that affect him? Rivas had just handed everything over—he could have stalled and made her get a court order first. If Riordan didn't have a few friends he wouldn't know what was going on around here.

Johnny MacAlister. He never wanted to hear that name again. The man almost made a fool out of him, blowing that bust the way he did. Pressure, Dan had told his contacts in the media. The man was under too much pressure. And when his wife accepted that . . . good thing for him MacAlister didn't bring the job home. As smart a cop as his wife was . . . if she approached this with her head . . . Damn, MacAlister could have cost him his career. There was no way the truth could come out now. Not with Holmes dead. Not with his initial statement destroyed. Sully and Lefty were first on the scene and they were from the old neighborhood. They'd never tell.

And Crosby? He was furious when he'd found out Riordan was conducting long-term investigations while he hid in his office. Even angrier when he understood the position their investigations put him in, confirming that crack cocaine was hitting the streets of Chicago while he was still insisting that it wasn't anything Middle America should be concerned about, that there was nothing here more serious than heroin, and that problem was not spreading to the suburbs.

Luckily, Crosby had already compromised himself when he

walked in after that Lopez raid. Danny boy asked him to leave the room for a few minutes so he could "think things through." Riordan knew that when he went back in, the cash count would be different, but a quarter of a million in thousands? Crosby had left the department a hell of a lot sooner than he had planned to, one hell of a lot richer, too.

If the superintendent had found out that they were dealing with that kind of money, and those quantities of shit, he would have demanded an accounting. If that had come out, there was no telling what Crosby might have done to save his own ass.

Riordan hadn't profited. He had run a clean shop and kept his men honest and tried to staunch the flow of drugs coming into the city. He had risked everything when nobody in the administration was willing to acknowledge that anything was wrong. Because of what he'd done under Crosby, when he was appointed vice deputy the teams and the tactics were already in place. He looked like an administrative genius when he took over Dan's command and showed everyone the level of narcotics activity on the street and the extent of the crack cocaine trade. If the mayor was looking around for a new superintendent, what better choice? But if everything became public because of MacAlister . . . he could kiss this job good-bye.

Riordan went to the telephone. "Say, Danny, guess who went to see Rivas today." He listened for a minute. "The term is Hispanic, Dan, Hispanic." He listened again. "Marti MacAlister, Johnny's wife. That homicide cop who solved the MacDonnough case. You know, the one they said couldn't be solved?"

Dan had really sweated the MacAlister case, called him in, insisted that it go down as a suicide. At the time, Riordan had been too concerned about covering his own ass to wonder why. Since then, the question had intrigued him. Whatever the reason, Crosby had had as much interest in keeping everything quiet as Riordan did.

Riordan listened again. "Jeez, Danny, clean up your language. That isn't politically correct. African-American, Danny. That's what it is now. You been away from the department too long." He smiled. "I'll keep you informed."

* * *

Diablo watched as Joe Riordan pulled up to the gate at the parking garage where he kept his car. Riordan showed a pass to the guard, then pushed a card in a slot to raise the gate. Again, the shiny blue Caprice was out of reach.

Inside, there was a guard on each floor. Two days ago, Diablo had made it to the second floor before being caught and escorted outside. The guard had threatened to call the police but it was the end of his shift and he didn't want the inconvenience.

It would be easier to get to the car while it was parked at police headquarters, but everything was out in the open. There wouldn't be enough time to hook up the bomb.

15

When Marti and Vik requested a meeting with Lieutenant Dirkowitz the next day and Vik added that it was personal, the lieutenant suggested that they go out to lunch at the Mariner, a local restaurant near the lake with great seafood. Every year the Mariner put on a fish-fry fundraiser for the high school, and Marti had eaten there many times with Ben.

Today, as she sat near the window, the sailboats that dotted the lake during the summer were sheltered in slips in the harbor, their tall masts bare. Seagulls, impervious to snow and cold, wheeled in wide circles, wings fluttering in updrafts of wind. The lieutenant made small talk while they ate chef's salads and New England clam chowder. Over coffee he paused, looking from one of them to the other. Marti filled him in on their activities in Chicago, beginning with Cantor's death.

"I'm glad you took the time to explain all of this," the lieutenant said. "I got a call last night from Vice Deputy Joseph Riordan suggesting that maybe I could keep you two busier in Lincoln Prairie."

"He called?" Vik said.

Dirkowitz nodded. Marti expected Vik to jump right in and ask how he responded, but for once, Vik kept his mouth shut.

"Interesting man, Riordan," the lieutenant said. "He spoke very slowly, enunciating each word."

Marti smiled as Dirkowitz mimicked the vice deputy. She had never witnessed it, but she could recall Johnny describing Riordan as condescending.

"I don't know if Riordan thinks we're retarded up here or just stupid, but I decided to be polite and not ask. I told him that what you and Vik do on your own time is your own business." As he leaned back, his hand closed around the salt shaker, a substitute for the hand grenade he kept on his desk.

"Riordan implied hysterical female, emotionally unbalanced, potentially trigger happy, grudge-bearing, vengeful." As he spoke he rubbed his thumb along one side of the salt shaker. "I thought most of it sounded more like Jessenovik." The lieutenant smiled. "Vik probably just shows you his good side, Marti. There are those of us who have heard about his days of high school glory playing hockey. I hear his dad made a notch for every head he split open."

This was the first time Marti had heard this. "And he looks so benevolent."

"That's how his nose got bent."

Vik scowled but said nothing.

"In any case, I'm glad you came to me with this, and I'm glad you're working on it together. I did a little asking around of my own. I haven't got any answers yet, but it seems that everything surrounding your husband's death was pretty cut and dried, at least as far as the superintendent and his cronies were concerned.

"Now I won't presume to suggest what I think you and Jessenovik should do when you're off duty. Nor will I say anything when you want time off, provided you take care of my shop first. I will say that I cannot imagine either of you behaving unprofessionally no matter what the circumstance or provocation, and your coming to me indicates that you intend to proceed with this in a responsible manner. I expect you to keep me abreast of whatever else I need to know. If necessary, we can assess whatever you find out and determine how to proceed."

That said, he banged the salt shaker on the table. End of lunch, end of meeting.

Vik looked ready to say something but Marti shook her head.

"Sorry you got that phone call first, Sir," she said.

"If you had waited any longer to come to me, I'd agree with you. Oh, and good work on the old bones we found at that explosion site. All's quiet, and we've bought enough time to wait for the forensic reports."

They had worked on leads all morning. "We've checked everything we can think of and there's nothing on record, Sir." Vik said. "Probably somebody who died a hundred years ago."

"I've heard about the pool," the lieutenant said.

Everybody in the precinct was taking bets on who the old bones might have been.

On the way back to the precinct, Vik said, "So, we're going to talk to this snitch tonight."

"Right."

"You think it's anything?"

"It's a snitch. Ski said Manuelito's name jumped right out at him. So, we'll see."

"You know this Manuelito?"

"Everybody in the district knows Manuelito."

Wednesday night, Marti and Vik drove to Chicago, exiting on Peterson heading east to an upscale neighborhood. When she found the address, Marti circled the block several times, snagging a parking place when someone pulled out.

As they walked half a block, Marti explained, "Manuelito, Little Manuel, had a companion, Big Manuel. I think big versus little might have been a joke between them because Big Manuel was the smaller of the two. One night they witnessed a gang-related shooting. We kept them under wraps and they testified. The jury convicted. One night a bunch of guys jumped them. Big Manuel didn't make it."

"Things like that are what keep people from speaking up," Vik said. "This is a nice neighborhood. Did you ever work here?"

"No. I requested my last assignment where the action was. We had the second highest homicide rate in the city."

Each of the houses, two-story, brick, had tall fences between them to prevent access to the rear. Manuelito's house had a steel door with security bars. There were more bars at the windows, upstairs and down. Marti gave the bell a series of rings, then rapped on the door in the pattern Manuelito had described.

"Detectives MacAlister and Jessenovik," she said when he came to the door. They held their shields a short distance from a peephole. Keys turned, chains clanked, and bolts slid for almost a minute before a large Hispanic man who looked at least sixty admitted them. He checked the street before closing the door and went through the lock ritual again.

"How's it going?" Marti asked. "Any problems since you've been here?"

"Shhh . . . " Manuelito cautioned, as if whoever he snitched on could hear him. "I don't think they've found out where I live. We settled Mannie's estate. If I'm careful, I don't have to work."

Marti turned to Vik. "Last place Manuelito lived in got burned down."

"The old man upstairs, he dies," Manuelito said, alternately wringing his hands and running his fingers through his hair. "Sit, sit, please sit."

All of the furniture was placed against the walls, away from the windows, which were hung with heavy curtains.

"You sit, Manuelito," Marti said. "Take it easy for a minute, relax, you're making me nervous."

"What is it that you want? If they are watching, they will think that I am telling you something again."

"But you do tell us many things."

"I used to; what I hear in the neighborhood, who is stealing, who is selling dope, but no more. Now I don't go out of the house. Even the groceries are delivered." He gestured toward the windows. "You see the curtains. I never open them. I see nothing. There is no way now to see someone get killed and tell you how he dies so that his killer can be brought to justice. Manny and I, we are together for thirty-one years." He folded his arms. "So, now I see nothing. Maybe, one day soon, I die."

"Tell me what you told Officer Holmes," Marti said, hoping she was right in guessing that DaVon had been here.

He smoothed his hair. "I . . . I . . . How do you know?"

"He was here a couple of weeks ago, wasn't he? What did you tell him?"

"He is dead!"

"Tell me! Word for word."

Manuelito clutched the arms of the chair and looked around the room. "He is looking for someone."

"Who?"

"He did not know."

"What *did* he know?"

"That he wanted to talk with a friend of mine who used to live in the old neighborhood when I did, before they kill Manny."

"What's your friend's name?"

Manuelito shrank back, shaking his head. "The last time I tell, someone dies."

"Maybe, if you tell this time, they won't."

"Fayesta," he whispered. "His name is Fayesta LaVerne. He lives on the south side now, near Ninety-first. That is all I know."

"Where does he hang out?"

"Where there are others like himself." Manuelito gave them the name of a bar, and when pressed, a description of Fayesta. Marti gave him her card.

An hour later Marti and Vik were parked on the south side.

"A transvestite bar," Vik said. "We are not going inside."

"Just watch and wait. If Fayesta is in there, he'll show."

She cut off the engine for a few minutes and the windows began to fog up. Snow, pockmarked with gravel and splattered with mud, lined the curbs. On the sidewalks, pedestrian traffic had packed the snow down.

"Nothing like winter in the city," Marti said. "So much pollution up there I bet the snow isn't even clean when it's coming down."

After about forty-five minutes, which Marti spent letting the car warm up, then turning off the engine, a tall hooker wearing a dark miniskirt and a waist-length fur jacket left the bar.

Vik rolled down the window. "Hey, Fayesta?"

"Yes, honey." Leaning down, he looked in at Vik. "Say, I'll bet y'all really like to get it on."

Marti showed Fayesta her badge.

"Cops! Hey look, y'all called me over here. I ain't said nothin' incriminating."

"We just want to talk to you for a few minutes," Marti said.

Vik stepped out of the car so Fayesta could get in on the passenger side. He got in the backseat.

Fayesta batted long fake eyelashes and gave Marti a practiced pout. "I truly ain't done a thing. Why y'all call me like that? What you want?"

"Talk to any narcs lately?" Marti asked.

"Narcs? I'm clean. Been clean since eighty-nine."

"The year Manny died."

Fayesta crossed his legs, causing his skirt to hike up. "Good people, Manny. How you know him?"

"I get around." Marti decided that Fayesta's shoulder length hair wasn't a wig, then wondered about the breasts. The jacket really bulged. She tried not to wonder about the men who would pick up Fayesta tonight.

"You talk to any cops lately?"

"Ain't been in no trouble for close to two years. Not one soliciting charge. Quiet out here. You keep your business to yourself, folks don't butt in. Ain't had nothing to do with no cops."

"What about maybe three years ago? You talk to a narc then?"

"Come on now, give me a break. How I remember something that far back." He clasped his hands together, twisting the scarf around his neck.

"A cop named MacAlister?"

"Who are you? What do you want?"

"Just asking," Marti said.

"No. Ain't never talked to no narc. Never talked with this Mac, Mac . . . "

"MacAlister."

"Right. Ain't never talked with him." He reached for the door handle. "You ain't got no right comin' here talkin' to me like this. I ain't even been picked up for nothing in over a year. Harassment, that's what it is."

"Fayesta," Marti said. "I don't work here any more. I work homicide in Lincoln Prairie now."

"You ain't no Chicago cop?"

"No. But I was."

"Lincoln Prairie? Where the hell is that? Iowa?"

"About sixty miles north of here."

"Oh. What you want with me?"

"I want to know what my husband talked with you about. My name's MacAlister." Marti handed Fayesta her card. "You think of what it was, you let me know." On a hunch, she said, "He told me you were one of his snitches."

"Why did he say that?" Fayesta didn't say it wasn't true.

"He looked out for his snitches, Fayesta. I'll look out for you, too."

Fayesta jerked open the door and slammed it as he got out. He tossed the scarf over his shoulder, then stumbled as his stiletto heel caught on a patch of ice on the sidewalk.

"Nothing to do but wait it out," Marti said. "We don't want to scare him away."

As they headed for home, Vik said, "What next?"

"I'm about two ideas short of a plan," Marti said. "Why not do what we always do, begin at the perimeter and work our way in. Let's take tomorrow off and go to the annex and check out arrest records."

"Sounds good." Vik rubbed his hands together, anticipating stacks of paper and hours of notetaking.

"We'll check out Fayesta. Johnny's name won't be on many of the big busts, but if we pull Murphy, since he was their sergeant, and flag the major busts, the odds are good that Johnny was involved. If what Leotha says holds up, most of Johnny's arrests should be street busts."

"And *Lope,*" Vik said. "I bet there are dozens of records with some variation of that." His voice was tinged with excitement. "Maybe we should pay this Riordan a visit while we're there, especially since he took the time to call the lieutenant."

"Interesting, isn't it," Marti agreed. "I wonder if Rivas suggested he call."

"Good cop, bad cop?" Vik said.

"Why not." She didn't trust either of them. "Those covert operations, the investigations nobody knew about, they have to play in all of this somehow."

"We're going to have to contact the first unit on the scene, and DaVon and Julian's partners, too, once we know enough to ask the right questions."

"Will they talk with us?"

"I don't know."

C H A P T E R

16

There was nothing imposing about police headquarters at Eleventh and State. A gray-brick facade extended several stories up, topped by red brick. Marti and Vik pushed on the glass doors and walked in from the street.

Marti recognized the uniform at the desk in the lobby.

"Stretch. How you doing?"

"MacAlister! Long time no see."

She introduced Vik.

"What brings you here?"

"We're going to the annex."

The records and files section was on the fourth floor of the annex. Marti thought about seeing Johnny's name at the top of a report and reading through it, gleaning bits and pieces of information that might tell her . . . what? Probably little or nothing. It was more a matter what she might surmise based on what she knew about the street and about being a narc.

"Why don't you take Johnny's," she said to Vik. Nothing could be worse than looking at that photograph, but her gut rebelled against the idea of getting this close to Johnny's work. She had a bitter taste in her mouth. She and Johnny had kept too many of the details of their work to themselves. She thought they did it to create a space where their lives were exactly as they wanted them to be—family, home, church, a few friends—a place where the insanity of the job couldn't touch them. Whatever the reason, her need to distance herself from Johnny's narc activities was as strong now as it had been then.

Vik signed out the files, looking at the unbound stacks of paper with an expression close to glee and hugging them to his chest as if someone would snatch them away. He watched without comment as Marti took out a bottle of Mylanta and shook half a dozen tablets into her hand.

Marti went through Fayesta's arrest records first, writing down the dates of the three drug busts. "There hasn't been anything in over a year. I wonder why not."

"Probably like she says. Nobody cares what goes on at that bar. Where was she before?"

"North side. Not that far from where Manuelito lives now."

They scanned the printed sheets all morning—name, sex, race, arrest charge, arresting officer, judge, disposition—without finding anything in common between DaVon and Cantor's arrest records, without finding any mention of Fayesta or anyone named *Lope* or any similar name. By noon, Vik had compiled a list of seventy-six perhaps named in both Cantor's and DaVon's reports. None of them was also on Johnny's, nor were any of Johnny's arrests also on theirs.

What Leotha had told her held up, Marti thought. For the most part, Johnny's arrests were minor. That made it easy for the department to downplay his death when he died. The major busts on the other narcs' reports were impressive. Johnny had probably helped set most of them up. If there was a pattern, it was that most involved suburban dealers buying drugs to take out of the city.

"Did Johnny have a personal stake in this?" Vik asked.

"His sister. She got into drugs and left home." They had never turned up any trace of her. Johnny was convinced she was dead.

The records they checked in the morning went back three to six months before Johnny's death. After breaking for lunch, they worked back as far as a year.

"Soda break," Marti said, a little after two, "or Murine?" Her eyes were burning. They both applied eyedrops.

"We'd better start checking out Lope, Lopes, Lopez and whatever," Vik said.

Again they came up empty. Even though she knew better than to expect anything, Marti was disappointed. There was too much she didn't know and might never be able to find out. When Johnny died, and the department "took care of its own," only the

Boys from Bridgeport were protected. Whatever happened the night Johnny died, not a word about their clandestine investigations ever came out. No matter how Johnny died, Riordan stepped over his grave to get into that office. How dare he suggest to Lieutenant Dirkowitz that she ought to stay home. How dare he imply that she was "unstable." How dare he? She would show him just how unstable she was.

Marti and Vik returned to the front desk. "Now we'd like to see Riordan. No appointment."

Stretch shrugged and picked up the phone. In a few seconds he motioned to them. "Well, the man will see you." He seemed as surprised as Marti was.

Riordan was at his desk when they arrived in his office. He didn't get up, extend his hand, or speak. He just sat there with the tips of his fingers touching his chin. Marti motioned Vik to one chair and sat in the other.

Johnny used to call Riordan Little Big Man. He looked older than Marti remembered, not just because his hair was graying at the temples. There was a weariness in the way his shoulders slumped that had replaced the energy she remembered. She decided to wait him out and make him speak first.

"So? What brings you here?" He sounded annoyed.

Marti wanted to really get on his nerves. "The way your narcs are dying these days. I've decided to take a closer look at what happened to Johnny."

"Look, MacAlister. Your husband put a gun to his head and pulled the trigger. You saw the pictures. He blew his brains out."

Marti refused to react. "I can understand your position. So much was going on in your unit then. But I don't believe that's the way it went down, and I intend to find out what did happen."

Riordan leaned back, appraising her. "If this is some kind of delayed reaction, Marti, if you're experiencing some new emotional difficulties dealing with this, I'm sorry."

That wasn't going to work either. "You know, Sir, reports seem to be a big problem in your department. When I looked at Johnny's arrest records, it was as if someone just falsified them. When I look at the busts I know he was involved in, he's not even mentioned. Key reports concerning his death are missing. You have big problems there, Sir. Big problems."

From the expression on Riordan's face, Marti knew he thought Johnny brought at least some of the job home. Good. There was no reason why he should know otherwise.

Riordan flushed. "Any peace officer in the state can come in here and access our files, but Chicago problems are dealt with by Chicago cops, and you don't work here anymore, remember that. This is out of your jurisdiction."

Marti stood up. "Don't get so emotional about it, Sir."

Vik was actually smiling as they left.

"Better watch that," Marti said. "Your face might break."

Late that night, when everyone else was in bed and the house was quiet, Marti went down to the kitchen. Without turning on the light she sat at the table, close enough to the window to feel the coolness of the air outside. A storm that had stalled over Iowa was beginning to move in. Snowflakes drifted down, not enough for any immediate accumulation, but the forecast was for four to six inches by tomorrow afternoon. It seemed so calm, so quiet. The wind had blown so hard and strong for so many days that without it the tree branches seemed abnormally still. Winter. It used to be her favorite time of year.

She felt tired. Her head hurt, and her shoulders ached from hunching over those reports all day. They had spent so much time accomplishing so little. How would she arrive at the truth? Trust your instincts, Johnny would say. Had she let him down, doing nothing these past three years? Was doing this now, when it seemed too late, what Johnny would want? Did he just want to rest in peace?

As she watched, the storm intensified until wet snow covered the windowsill.

"Chestnuts," Johnny would say, evoking memories of their childhood. Not hot chestnuts roasting on an open fire—hot chocolate spiced with vanilla and nutmeg, popcorn made in a cast-iron pot with sugar added to caramelize it, the round kerosene heater in the center of the living room that was turned off when it was time for bed.

"Chestnuts." She was the only one who could always interpret what Johnny's one-worders meant. Somehow, she would work her way through Cantor's one-worders, too.

17

Crosby waited until midnight before going out. He zipped up a black parka, pulled his watchcap over his ears, and wrapped a scarf around his chin and nose. His mittens were large enough for one of his throwaway guns to fit inside. He put another street acquisition into his pocket, a home-made silencing device. Armed and safe, Crosby went into the streets of Chicago.

The wind slapped tiny wet flakes of snow in his face as soon as he stepped into the cold. A bus pulled away from the kiosk with four passengers inside. A cab turned the corner, slowed as the driver observed him on the almost deserted street, and when he showed no interest, sped past.

Crosby walked a familiar beat. It was almost one o'clock when he reached Division Street and made a random sweep of the alleys, gradually moving closer to an area where there were several gay bars.

As Crosby cut through an alley, a man in a coat that came almost to his ankles turned into the alley and walked toward him. Five five, Crosby estimated, unable to judge his weight. Crosby stepped behind a Dumpster, feeling sweat dampen his armpits. Fruits shouldn't be allowed to walk the streets, he thought. They needed to be locked up somewhere, all of them.

As the man neared the Dumpster, Crosby stepped out, bumped into him and said, "Hey, watch where the fuck you're going."

"Sorry."

Up close, Crosby saw that this one wasn't even old enough to shave. He gave him a shove.

"Hey, look man . . ."

"You propositioning me?" Crosby said.

"No man, hey, I was just—"

He stopped, staring at the gun in Crosby's hand. "Hey, hey man, look, I . . . I . . ."

Crosby grabbed the kid by the arm and pressed the muzzle of the gun against his neck. "There's those of us who don't appreciate being hustled by the likes of you."

The boy breathed hard through his mouth. His eyes, wide with fear, were a watery blue.

"Trash," Crosby said. "Get outta here."

As the boy ran, Crosby fitted the silencer on the gun and fired above the kid's head. Hearing the pop, the kid dove into a pile of garbage bags.

Laughing, Crosby turned and walked the other way. His heart was beating so fast he couldn't catch his breath. He stopped, leaning against a building, clutching his chest and bending forward. Too much excitement for an old man. But he wasn't old. Not yet. He wasn't old.

Across the street, a man came out of a bar. In a minute, another man followed. They spoke, then walked off together. It was just like what happened that night. He just stopped for a quick drink. He had walked a long way. He was thirsty, that's all. He didn't know it was a gay bar until all the fruits began staring at him. When the fruit sitting next to him smiled, he left without finishing his beer. Then, when he walked through that alley, the kid had come up to him and asked for money. "For doing what filthy things?" he had asked. The kid looked so scared when he pulled out the gun. Instead of running, he had grabbed it. He looked so surprised when it went off.

Crosby gulped in deep breaths of cold air. It was self-defense. Nobody knew. Nobody would ever know.

18

Marti woke up before the alarm went off Thursday morning. A word danced on the edges of her memory, something she had dreamed, something she could not quite recall. This had happened before. She took slow deep breaths, relaxing until she was almost asleep again. Manuelito? No, that wasn't it, but something Spanish. *Chicomuno.* That was the word, but what was it? Not food. A singing group? She couldn't remember. *Chicomuno.* The alarm buzzed and she got up.

The storm had dropped three inches of snow. When Marti left for work the wind had quieted and the snow, still falling steadily, had blanketed everything in a cold, white silence that she found soothing. She spent Thursday morning in court with Vik. The State's attorney liked their performance with Attorney Allen so much that she called them in again as rebuttal witnesses.

Marti tried not to think about the word, but wondered what had teased it into her memory. On the way to the precinct she said it aloud, then tried to find it, or something like it, in a Spanish-American dictionary. "Chicomuno," she said. "Chico and the man. Chico." A name?

Then she remembered Johnny with the headphones on, listening to salsa, getting her to dance, and saying "chicomuno" everytime the background singers shouted something else. When she repeated it, he smiled and kissed her and she forgot. Two weeks later he was dead.

Important? Probably not. But it wasn't one of his one-worders, either. His mood was lighter that night. He was less preoccupied.

His hands caressed her hips as they danced, his lips moved from her earlobe to her neck. And then that mood was gone, and he was quiet, almost to the point of brooding, until he died.

She got out the Chicago telephone book, turned to "M." Munaz, Munes, Muniz, Munnas, Munoz. Chico Munoz? Her instincts said yes.

As they drove back to Chicago, Vik stared out the window in silence.

"Getting used to the traffic?" Marti asked.

"There is no such thing as rush-hour traffic anymore. As soon as everyone who has volunteered for this insanity makes it to work, the truckers take over, along with everyone who lives in the suburbs and thinks there still is a rush hour."

When they reached the annex, the clerk said, "Back again?"

Marti wondered if he would call upstairs to Riordan and let him know they were there.

Under Munoz, Vik had seventeen narcotics arrest records pulled, then flipped through them before passing them to her. "Johnny, Cantor, and DaVon were not involved in any of these."

Marti looked without finding anything either. "Doesn't mean they weren't there."

"Unfortunately," Vik agreed.

"Let's cross-reference them with our variations of Lope."

Vik groaned.

"What's the matter, Jessenovik? Getting tired of all these wonderful, exciting, fascinating stacks of paper?"

In another hour and a half they narrowed it down to three weeks before Johnny died. "Bingo," Marti said. "Pittman Lopez. Now we just have to find out if Lopez is important and how Munoz fits in. We might even come up with another reason to go through more reports."

Vik groaned again.

"First we need to find out what these two are up to these days and have a little talk with them," Marti said.

It didn't take long to find out that Pittman Lopez was in Milwaukee. Munoz was dead. His body had been found three weeks after Johnny died, but according to the coroner's report, both men had died at about the same time.

19

Marti and Vik worked on a routine death investigation most of Friday morning, then filled Lieutenant Dirkowitz in on the lack of progress with the skeletal remains. That done, they drove to Wisconsin to see Pittman Lopez.

They had stayed at the annex long enough to find out that after numerous arrests in Chicago, Lopez had moved his drug dealing operation farther north with similar results. He was doing time now for possession of two dime bags of marijuana, probably for personal use. Marti took Interstate 94 to the Ryan Road exit and drove west to the Milwaukee County Jail, a medium security facility. Wisconsin had gotten the brunt of yesterday's storm. Acres of farmland stretched to the left and right of the road with undisturbed snow almost reaching the tops of the fenceposts.

As they approached the red-brick building surrounded by double barbed-wire fences, Vik said, "Jail. Some guys will do just about anything for a little male bonding."

They checked their weapons and a corrections officer took them upstairs to the visitor's room. A few minutes later, Pittman Lopez came in wearing a green jumpsuit. Short, thick-necked and muscular, he looked like he spent a lot of his jail time lifting weights.

"Yeah, man," he said, pulling a chair over to the table. "I don't know why you come to see me. I don't owe the State of Illinois nothing." Arms folded, he leaned back in his chair.

"We wanted to talk with you about one of your friends, Chico Munoz," Marti said.

Lopez seemed wary, but not hostile.

"Last I heard, Munoz was dead," he said.

"You got busted together in a raid about three years ago," Marti said. "Tell me about it."

"What's in it for me?"

Marti shrugged. "Nothing much," she said. "Cigarette money, maybe."

Lopez gave her just a hint of a smile as he spoke. "What the hell . . . Aah. What you say your name is? MacAlister?" He leaned back and gave Marti a broad, gold-capped grin. "Now we get to it, Miss Officer, Ma'am. I know who you are. Maybe we can deal."

"Maybe."

"What you want to know?"

"Descriptions of as many officers at the raid as you can recall."

"That will cost you a lot more than cigarettes."

Marti nodded to Vik and stood up, calling his bluff. She only dealt with cons on her terms.

"You bring me my kid and I talk to you," Lopez said.

"Your kid?"

"Yeah, my old lady got a kid since I been in here. She's a crack addict. State got the kid." Lopez's grin seemed mocking this time. "You the big shot homicide dick, Officer, Ma'am. You get me my kid."

His eyes betrayed him. He really did want to see his child.

"Illinois DCFS?" Marti asked.

Still grinning, he nodded.

Marti was on the phone to her friend Denise Stevens, a juvenile probation officer, as soon as they got downstairs.

"Lopez might not know anything," Vik said. "What he does know might not be worth anything."

Chicomuno, Marti thought. It meant something. She wanted to find out what. "Denise says she'll get right on it."

"Another hunch?" Vik said. He did not like words like hunch and professed to mistrust intuition. Although he used both as often as she did, he preferred to insist it was sound reasoning and logic.

"Maybe," she said.

He looked at her for a moment, then said, "What the hell."

20

As Riordan stared at the polished surface of his desk, he reached beneath it with a letter opener and made small gouges where nobody could see them. This morning's meeting with the other vice deputies and the superintendent had been a fiasco. Rourke, of all people, suggested that maybe he couldn't control his men. Like he needed that from somebody who hadn't left his office in two years. What did Crosby's buddy Rourke know about anything?

He controlled his men one hell of a lot better than Crosby had ever done. He even got off his ass and rode with his men now and then. Crosby hid out in this office for six years. Never did nothing. Never knew what was going on and got rid of anyone who tried to tell him. Control of his men. He gave the letter opener a twist, heard the wood yield.

There was a knock, and Riordan threw the letter opener on his desk just as Frank Murphy came in. Damn, but Murphy was becoming a fat son of a bitch. Fat and lazy. Careless, too. Spending too much time with that little Italian bride of his.

Riordan pointed to a chair. "What's going on with your unit, Frank? Two men down in less than two weeks."

"DaVon Holmes went down during a well-planned, well-reconnoitered drug bust. We made out big time. Got the drugs, a major dealer—"

"And a dead cop. The superintendent doesn't like having two dead cops, and I don't like losing two good cops. They didn't come any better than Cantor and Holmes. And we didn't get anything when Cantor went down. Nothing but trouble. You didn't even know what was going on."

"Cantor was working with the DEA."

"And they didn't know what was going on, either. I don't need anybody else working under you to make any more field decisions. You got that, Frank?" The only reason Murphy was still here was Dan Crosby. "If anyone else in your unit screws up, you're all out of vouchers. Now you'd better get your mind off your little signorina and get your ass back out on the street."

"Joe, I—"

"You don't just work days, ten to three, Frank. Your men are on the street twenty-four hours a day, and that's where you'd better be, and the little woman better get used to that, fast."

"Joe . . . "

"I know where you've been and for how long every day and night since you got married. Two of your men went down. Get the connection?"

Murphy's Adam's apple bobbed as he nodded.

"And somebody better give up something on Leotha Jamison, because it's coming down to your ass or hers."

After Murphy left, Riordan wondered who was watching him. Somebody wanted his job. Was it someone sitting at the table with him at last night's banquet? Someone at the meeting this morning? Did the mayor have a crony who wanted to see his kid sitting here? It was probably someone Riordan himself had handpicked. There was no loyalty. Any suggestion of weakness on his part and their jobs were on the line, too. They'd move like a pack of dogs to a stronger mentor.

As soon as Murphy took care of Jamison, he'd be reassigned—to Shakespeare, District Fourteen, Area Five, a district where there was lot of action. Someplace where there was no time to stay at home. Frank kept himself as far away from the action as he could. He needed to work where that was impossible, so that everyone could see what kind of a cop he really was.

Riordan twisted the letter opener as it splintered the wood. Rourke had the balls to suggest that some of his units were out of control. Rourke didn't know what out of control was. He had never worked under Dan Crosby.

* * *

An hour later Riordan cruised past the office building where Crosby lived, noted that the lights were on, and went a few blocks west to pick up some Chinese food.

"Where the hell were you after midnight last night, Dan?"

"Huh?" Crosby stopped scooping fried rice onto his plate.

"I came by last night."

"Oh. Bar a few blocks from here."

At last week's staff meeting Rourke had mentioned seeing Crosby duck down an alley near Belmont and Clark, a known gay area. Rourke headed Vice. Crosby was getting too old to go gay bashing, but if Rourke wanted him to get that message, he'd have to deliver it himself.

"I thought maybe that stewardess was in town and you were at her place." Like other women Crosby had mentioned, Riordan had never met her. "You two haven't broke up already, have you?"

"You know me, love 'em and leave 'em."

"Come on. You haven't been seeing her more than a couple of months. At least keep one of these bimbos long enough to intro- duce her around."

Crosby ripped open a packet of soy sauce and poured it over his rice. "She's never here. What good is she?"

"That why you're out bar hopping? Looking for broads?"

Crosby shook his head and popped a batter-fried butterfly shrimp into his mouth.

"You're not that far from Belmont and Clark. Close enough for a cab."

Crosby swallowed too fast and began coughing. Riordan half rose from his chair.

"No, no." Crosby shook his head. "I'm okay." He spoke in a whisper, cleared his throat and tried again. "Went down the wrong way." He wiped his eyes with the back of his hand and gulped down half a glass of water. "How's things with you, Joey? You're not staying late because MacAlister's wife's been snooping around?"

Riordan maintained eye contact. "She's a little upset about the missing evidence."

Crosby flushed.

Riordan recalled seeing Crosby at the cemetery the night Mac-Alister died, red in the face and chewing out the homicide cop because the bullet had not yet been found. "I don't want there to be any doubt about what happened here tonight," he had said. When the reports from the first uniforms on the scene went missing two weeks later, Crosby had ranted for half an hour about it, calling everyone from the vice deputy of violent crimes to the superintendent.

Crosby emptied a can of beer.

"So, Joey. How much you giving up this time when you get your pockets picked by Margo's lawyer?"

"Ain't much left," Riordan admitted, without adding that he had figured out a few tricks for hiding most of what was there. "I'm paper poor," he admitted with a wink.

"I can make you an offer you can't refuse. Double what you're making now."

"For what? All the more to give to the next bimbo."

Crosby helped himself to another shrimp, finishing it in two bites. "Joey, you gotta start listening to me. You should be working here, talking with my financial advisor . . . "

"Financial advisor? What the hell kind of settlement they give you when you retired?"

Crosby hesitated.

Riordan smiled. The quarter million Crosby skimmed sat between them like a fat, happy little voucher that Riordan could always call in.

Crosby cleared his throat. "In this business, Joey, people like dealing with an ex-cop; gives them a sense of security."

Riordan speared a shrimp and wagged it at Crosby in a small arc encompassing the room. "Security," he agreed.

"Just wait, Joey. Just wait 'til your birthday. Wait'll you see the surprise I got for you this year."

Last year it had been a ride on Crosby's new boat, with someone else doing the steering.

"You learn how to handle that rusty tub of yours yet?"

"Rusty tub? Joey, you know what that set me back? I'm learning. This year I'll take you out myself."

"No way. I liked having that young kid behind the wheel. He knew what he was doing. Got us out there, and brought us back in."

Dan chuckled. "Just wait until this year. No assistants. Just me and you." He leaned back and patted his stomach.

"So what's new in the world of narcotics?"

Once a cop . . . Riordan thought.

After Joey left, Crosby walked to the pay phone near the corner. He punched in a phone number and waited while it rang three times, then hung up and called again. "You find out where that Fayesta LaVerne hangs out?"

He opened his notebook to the most recent entry and felt uneasy just reading the name his friend in records had given him. Fayesta LaVerne. Why was MacAlister's old lady pulling arrest records?

"Thanks. You know that dope house you got on the north side?" He gave the address. "You really ought to close it down before Wednesday."

It was almost closing time when Crosby reached the bar on the far south side. He didn't like the neighborhood, even though the small brick houses along the street where he parked were a lot like those in the old neighborhood, except that they had a little more yard. A black man walked past with his dog. Crosby watched as the dog relieved itself in someone's yard and the man scooped it up. Too many coloreds here. Crosby checked the doors again, even though he had automatic locks.

He'd get a feel for the area tonight, so that when he called and made a date with this Fayesta . . .

The fruits were starting to leave the bars. He-shes, Crosby decided, as a tall one wearing a short fur jacket and miniskirt crossed the street in front of the car. A dark face peered into the window and paused. Crosby gripped the gun with one hand and held it low at his side. The fruit took two steps back and hurried away.

21

Marti awakened to the sound of someone tapping on her door. She lay still. Maybe they would go away.

"Ma?"

"Joanna." Marti opened her eyes, then sat up. "Come in. What's wrong?"

"It's eight in the morning. Did you miss roll call?"

"No, it's okay. I don't have to go in." Marti plumped her pillow. It seemed like weeks since she'd slept in. "Ahh. This feels wonderful."

"You're off on Saturday again? Two weeks in a row? Does this mean you can come to my game tonight?"

"I think so, if nothing comes up."

Joanna yawned and climbed in beside her.

"What time did you come in last night?" Marti asked. Sharon had waited up for Joanna and Lisa so that Marti could turn in.

"I made curfew."

"Midnight? Where did you and Chris go?"

"Roller-skating. Then we stopped for pizza."

Marti closed her eyes. "Be okay if you dated a few guys, instead of just one."

"Did you?"

"Uh-uh. Just your father."

"So what if I just date Chris?"

"Until I was sixteen, your dad and I only saw each other at school and in church. The closest we came to a date was when he walked me home."

"Things were different then, ma."

Marti smiled, remembering Momma and half the neighborhood watching or calling to them from the window. "Slower. We had time to become friends."

"Suppose I wanted to go on the pill?"

The pill? They hadn't been dating more than six months, had they? Joanna and Chris needed contraceptives? Chris? Could she be that easily deceived by a quiet, polite, studious young man with a great sense of humor—a jock, tall, great bod, perfect pecs, no acne . . . Had they? Already? "Things aren't that serious, are they?"

"Of course not."

Then why had Joanna asked?

"Chris has an older brother, ma. His mother keeps condoms in the medicine cabinet."

Condoms? The next time she saw Chris's mother at church she would have a lot more to talk about than how great the choir sounded. "We haven't had them over since . . . "

"New Year's Day. You had a hit-and-run and came home long enough to say hello."

At least she had made it home. And Chris, when was the last time she had seen him? She couldn't remember.

"Didn't you tell me the captain of the basketball team asked you out?"

"Oh ma, his father's a cop."

"Good." Maybe instead of stocking up on condoms his father counseled abstinence. "What's his name?"

"Dean."

"George Dean's kid?"

"Yeah."

Dean, married with two kids, had been reprimanded recently for a backseat rendezvous in his squad car while parked behind Dunkin' Donuts. "You don't want to date him."

"That's what I just said."

Contraceptives. Marti didn't feel up to this conversation. Peer pressure, that's what it was. "How many of your girlfriends are still virgins?"

Joanna giggled. "Half—maybe. I haven't taken a poll lately."

"At fifteen? Half?" She would have guessed about a third.

Maybe things weren't as bad as she thought. "I should have sent you to Carmel High School." Nuns still believed in abstinence, didn't they?

"Times have changed, ma."

No point in the usual arguments. The way Joanna worried about Marti's consumption of saturated fats, cholesterol levels, and caffeine intake, it was Marti's turn to overreact this time. "I heard there's a higher incidence of breast and cervical cancer if you become sexually active before your twenty-sixth birthday."

"Ma! Who said I was going to become sexually active?"

Marti knew she hadn't dozed off for a minute and missed something. "Then why are we talking about this?"

"Because some of the kids on the student council want to get up a petition to have contraceptives available at school without parental consent, and we decided to find out how our parents felt about it."

"But that's not what you asked me."

"Oh ma, I knew you'd be all for it if it was for somebody else. I wanted to know how you'd feel if it were me."

Had she flunked another parenting test? "Then let's talk about you and Chris. Do we need to have a talk about boys or dating or contraceptives or sex or teenage pregnancy or anything?"

"No."

"You would talk with me about this first and not just raid Chris's medicine cabinet, right?"

"Probably. If I was still underage."

Had she finally passed a parenting test?

Marti thought about getting up. It seemed strange sleeping in, a Saturday morning with nothing to do.

She curled up close to Joanna. "Remember getting in my bed when you were a little girl?"

"Ummm. Thanks."

"For what?"

"Not thinking that I'm still a kid."

Marti smiled. "Old folks child," Momma would say the next time she saw Joanna. If only Johnny could be here. When she was almost asleep, Joanna said, "Why did you and Daddy wait?"

Marti thought of the two of them, dancing—salsa, late at night while the children were sleeping. Everything was sweeter for the waiting. More intense. She touched Joanna's cheek, then touched her hair, seeing Momma, seeing herself, in Joanna's face. "We thought we had forever."

22

When Marti and Joanna got up, the house was quiet. Sharon and Lisa were shopping and Ben had taken Theo and Mike to brunch and an afternoon Bulls game. Ben had bought the tickets the first day they went on sale. Theo hadn't begun to get excited about seeing his first professional game until Thursday. When Ben picked him up last night, it was all he could talk about. Listening to him, Marti thought about Johnny's basketball trophies. She still wasn't sure about getting them out of storage.

While Marti browsed the weekend edition of the *News-Times,* Joanna made mushroom and cheese omelettes and toast with strawberry jam.

"More tea, ma?"

"Please. Rosehips." Joanna never drank that kind, so Marti had mixed it with Lipton for some caffeine.

"Didn't Daddy ever . . . feel different than you did about waiting?" Joanna asked, sitting down.

"I don't think so." Marti knew this was more important to Joanna than a survey on parental attitudes. She tasted her omelette. "Ummm. Delicious." Marti wasn't sure how Joanna got the fake eggs that came in little cartons to taste this good.

"Home was different for your dad than it was for me. His mother drank a lot, and he and his sister did most of the housecleaning while his father was at work." It was always such a dusty apartment, in need of sunshine and fresh air. "Nobody argued, at least not often, but they didn't laugh much either. Or discuss things like we did. He spent a lot of time at my house. I think we both wanted what my parents had."

"Grandma?"

"Momma was a sexy lady." Until she said it, Marti didn't realize she thought of her mother that way. Momma was a tall, large-boned woman. When she smiled there was a gap between her front teeth. Marti always thought of cooking smells when she thought of her—vanilla, cinnamon, oregano, sage.

"My daddy was a porter," Marti said, between bites of omelette. "He'd be gone for days. When he came home, Momma would have pots of greens and beans and turkey wings simmering on the stove. Momma would go to Miss Pearl's house and have her hair straightened with iron combs heated on the stove. And as soon as Daddy turned that corner, Momma would splash on this rose-scented toilet water that he brought back whenever he went to California."

Daddy was a slender man, not as tall as Momma, twelve years older, with gray hair. When he smiled, he looked younger. "He'd always bring me candy when he came home, and tell me how much he'd missed me and how pretty I was. Then Momma would put on Count Basie or Billie Holiday and I knew it was time for me to go stay with Miss Pearl for the rest of the day. A couple of Miss Pearl's ladies would be there getting their hair done. They'd get to smiling and giggling about Daddy being home. It didn't take me long to figure out why I had to stay there. That was what I wanted with your father, something worth waiting for, something worth spending time on, something to be enjoyed. You understand what I'm saying?"

Joanna pushed away from the table, brushing her long auburn hair away from her face. "You and Dad were happy, weren't you? You were happy together almost all the time. Do you think it would still be like that, if he was still here?"

"I think so."

Joanna pulled the curtain aside and looked out the window. Theo had filled the birdfeeder and sparrows were landing and taking off. "What about Ben?" she said.

"I don't know yet. Is that important?"

"Most of my friends, their parents are just—together, like it's no big deal. I want you to be happy, the way you were with Dad."

Marti wasn't sure that could happen. "I don't expect things to ever be quite that way again."

"Ben's really nice. And he's real good with Theo. Theo needs that."

Just as Joanna needed a dad. Could Ben be a father to her? Would Marti consider marrying him for that? "I think that even if things stay just the way they are with Ben and me, you could trust him as a friend."

When Joanna didn't answer, Marti went to her. "When my daddy came home, he always cut out paper dolls for me. He was the only daddy in the neighborhood who did. I was fourteen when he died. I still miss him. Your dad could not replace him, just as nobody can ever replace your dad. There are things that you have to put down, so that you can pick up something else. Your dad and I danced a lot. If there ever is someone else, we'll share something special, too, but it won't be the same. If you need a man to talk with, try Ben."

After breakfast, Marti went through her notes again. Then she called Vik. He agreed that they should talk with Fayesta again tonight, see if they could gain his confidence. Vik wanted to go to evening mass and have dinner with his wife, Mildred, first.

Next, Marti called Denise to find out if she had located Lopez's child. She got Denise's answering machine and left a message.

Joanna rushed in carrying her ice skates and gave Marti a quick kiss good-bye. Marti had the whole afternoon to herself, and the house was unusually quiet.

Marti called the couple in Boca Raton who had owned Mary's Place when it was the Home Run Inn. They had just returned from a trip to the Bahamas and confirmed what she already knew: the contractors who built it, when it was built. The two units upstairs were rented on lease and never for less than a year. None of the tenants had ever gone missing, and no one-night stands or any other immoral behavior was allowed. Just because the apartments were located above a bar did not mean that their establishment was frequented by prostitutes. Marti's ear felt numb by the time she hung up. The call relieved whatever guilt she'd been feeling about not putting in more time at work lately. She wondered how much longer it would be before Lincoln Prairie had another homicide. In four days they would tie the record.

It was eight-thirty at night when Vik met her at the precinct. They decided to check out Smitty and Irene, the two early birds at Mary's place, before going to Chicago to see Fayesta.

A uniform had tracked them both down at a bar about three blocks from where the explosion occurred. So far, Vik hadn't been able to catch either of them sober enough for an intelligent conversation. Marti and Vik were trying to catch them at home at a time when the booze might be wearing off.

"Maybe they never leave the bar," Vik said. "Maybe they just slide off the stool and sleep on the floor."

"We've only stopped by twice."

There was no answer when they went to the bungalow where Smitty rented a room. The three-story wood-framed house on the far northeast side of town where Irene lived reminded Marti of a haunted house the kids had visited last Halloween. The gate hung on one hinge and creaked when they pushed it open. Huge icicles hung from the gutters, pulling them away from the roof, and the downspout hung at an odd angle, swinging each time the wind blew. Marti slipped and slid to the front door. Only three houses on the block had their steps and sidewalks shoveled. The one Irene lived in wasn't one of them.

The hallway was lit, and cleaner than Marti expected. There was no trash, no odor of rotting garbage. On the second floor, flowerpots with plastic geraniums had been placed on either side of Irene's door.

A quiet voice answered when Marti knocked. When the door opened, a cat brushed past her legs. A small boy darted after it, swooping down to gather it into his arms. Marti noticed the cat's smoky gray fur first, then the bright yellow eyes. Then she looked at the boy, small for his age, with straight black hair and the bluest eyes she had ever seen.

"Padgett?" she said. "Is that you?"

"Yes, ma'am," the boy said in a small voice.

* * *

Marti made a call, and Denise Stevens came over right away. She was Marti's height and not more than ten pounds heavier. Unlike Marti, she wasn't comfortable with her size. Tonight, Denise wore a tentlike black coat and roller-brimmed felt hat with a scarf that tied under her chin.

Denise made a thorough inspection of the apartment, checking closets, drawers, cabinets. She was in with Irene, Padgett's mother, now behind the closed bedroom door. Marti wondered if Denise had been able to rouse her. Padgett seemed to huddle into himself as he sat on a sofa with bricks where the legs should have been. He shivered, even though the heat in the apartment was stifling. The gray cat rubbed against his legs and settled itself on his lap.

Padgett hadn't grown much since the last time Marti saw him over a year ago, when he was a runaway trying hard not to get caught. He still looked too thin. She remembered the little boy who hid with his friends in the abandoned library and went out into the darkness to protect them, and wondered if Padgett was still afraid of the dark. She felt like a traitor when she called Denise, even though she knew it was the right thing to do. When she hung up she asked Padgett if he was hungry, but he wouldn't answer. He hadn't said a word since. Marti wanted to hug him, to reassure him that everything would be okay, but she didn't know if anyone, even Denise, could make that happen, and she couldn't lie.

The radiator made little clanking sounds. Maybe it was cooling down. The place was so hot that someone had raised the window about an inch to let some cold air in. The apartment was tiny: two bedrooms, each just big enough for a single bed and a dresser; a living room and a kitchen crowded with appliances and a table with two chairs. There were two other apartments on this floor and two kitchenettes in the attic.

Denise came out of Irene's room, closing the door behind her. "Padgett, what are you having for supper?" she asked.

Padgett hugged himself tighter. "Hamburgers. And Spa-ghettiOs," he said, speaking just above a whisper.

"How long have you been with your mother?"

"Almost a year."

"Here?"

"Uh-huh."

Denise sat on the couch beside him. "Where do you go to school?"

"Couple blocks from here. Rogers Middle School."

"When I call them, how many days will they tell me you've missed since September?"

He thought for a minute. "Three. No, five. I had the flu."

"Did you see the doctor?"

"No. I don't have a card."

"Why are you back with your mom?"

His chin jutted out at a defiant angle. "I want to stay with her. She left my dad. He's the one I don't want to be with."

"Your mom can't take care of you."

"I'm eleven, I can take care of myself. We take care of each other."

"You seem to be doing all right," Denise agreed. "Does your mom smoke?"

"No."

"Does she get up at night and try to cook?"

"No, she . . . " he hesitated. "She burned a pot once. Now she wakes me up if she wants something."

"Does she always remember to do that?"

"Yeah." He came close to smiling. "She says I'm good company."

"When's a good time to talk with your mom?"

"Tomorrow. Before seven o'clock mass."

"Good. I need to talk with Detective MacAlister and Detective Jessenovik now."

Padgett started to get up.

"No. You stay here. We'll be talking about you. You might as well listen." Denise turned to Marti and Vik.

"I did what checking I could before I came over. Padgett has run away from seven foster homes since the last time we saw him. Right now he's been listed as a runaway for eleven months. This might not seem like the ideal placement for him, but he seems to have done a better job of placing himself than we have, and he's in a situation he's willing to stay in."

"You're going to let him stay here?" Marti asked.

"Yes."

Padgett scooted away from Denise. "You're lying to me so I won't run away."

"If you couldn't stay here, I'd take you with me now," Denise told him. "I'm going to come back and talk with you and your mom to find out how I can help you stay together. If you get sick again, you need to be able to see a doctor. And there will be some rules. You are going to come to my office two afternoons a week. Your mom is an alcoholic. That's hard even for adults to cope with. You need help with that."

Padgett ducked his head down. Denise took his chin in her hand and made him look at her. "It's not easy, Padgett, but it's okay. Drinking doesn't make her a bad person or a bad mom. There are other kids who live with alcoholics who can help you. This looks like a situation we can work with. Just don't get scared again and run away on me." When Denise put her arms around him, Padgett didn't pull away.

Outside, as they walked to their cars, Denise said, "Lopez saw his little girl today."

"Already?" Marti said. "How'd you manage that so fast?"

"You sounded like it was urgent. And I am an officer of the court. Lopez is quite the family man. Loves his kids. Likes his women young, too. This one's mother is sixteen and he's already turned her on to cocaine. I told him I'd try to get her into a decent rehab program. Sometimes it works. Who knows?"

"I owe you one," Marti said.

"No, I owe you. Many."

In the course of a recent investigation, Marti had found out that Denise and both of her sisters had been molested as children by Denise's stepfather. It was a difficult case, and Marti wasn't sure she wanted to know how Denise's family was doing, but she asked anyway.

"Belle's graduated to an extended care alcohol rehab program.

I never thought she'd stick it out, but so far so good. And Momma still has Terri's little girl, Zaar. She's in preschool now and you wouldn't believe the way that child talks."

"And Terri?" Marti said.

Denise shook her head. "She's not making any progress. The psychiatrist thinks she'll be institutionalized for quite a while."

Marti looked up and saw Padgett watching from the window. "You think you can help him? Hell of a life for a kid."

"Not as bad as some," Denise said. "I know a lot of kids who would trade places with him."

23

The chaplain for the Milwaukee County Jail called Marti late Sunday morning. Pittman Lopez wanted to see her. By two o'clock Vik and Marti were in a small visitor's room, sitting at a round table. The yellow walls looked recently painted and the dark tile floor was polished to a hard shine.

"They must make them work," Vik said. "On-the-job training, in jail. I bet they even pay them. For some of them, it must seem like some kind of reward. Their family comes and they can say 'Hey ma, I finally got a job.' "

Jails made Marti twitchy. "Couldn't pay me enough to work here," she said.

Lopez was escorted in a few minutes later. He looked from Vik to Marti, then watched as the guard closed the door. For a moment, he seemed dejected. Then he sighed. The chair scraped against the floor as he pulled it out and sat down, arms folded, muscles bulging beneath the green jumpsuit.

"My kid came to see me," he said. "Some probation officer brought her." He looked away for a minute, then gave Marti a belligerent stare. "I don't like owing no cop."

"So give me something and we'll call it even," Marti said.

"That bust you asked me about? Why you so interested in a narc raid? On account of your husband? We never knew he was a cop 'til his picture got in the paper. Man stung us so many times I shouldn't be telling you nothin'."

She thought Johnny was making street buys. What else did Leotha know that Johnny hadn't told his own wife? How many more surprises were there? Marti's stomach tensed and she wished she could reach for the antacid. Instead, she pulled out her notebook.

"Tell me about this raid, with Munoz."

"Munoz." Lopez's smile was more like a sneer. "Quiet little fucker. Just kind of there, around. Walked, too. Don't think I ever paid no attention to him 'til he walked after that raid. Knew somebody, the little bastard. Probably one of the cops at the raid."

It didn't sound as if Lopez connected Munoz with Johnny. Could anyone else have?

"Give me some names."

She flipped to the list she had taken from the arrest report. Lopez's recollections concurred.

"See any cops you recognized?"

"Sure. Sergeant Asshole was there—excuse me, Sergeant Murphy, now Lieutenant Murphy. You guys called him that, not me."

Marti kept her expression neutral as Lopez named DaVon Holmes, Riordan, Crosby, and half a dozen other officers whose names weren't on the report.

"That's it?"

"Yeah."

"How long were you dealing out of that house before they came in?"

According to the arrest sheet it was a routine bust, but with that many narcs involved off the record, it had to be bigger.

"Coupla months. I almost made it that time. I was selling to a dealer who was working the south and west suburbs. And I still don't know who they were sending in to make the buys." Lopez rubbed a heart-shaped tattoo on the back of his hand. "I almost made it, big time. Twelve kilos of cocaine." He looked at her and winked. "Quarter of a million dollars, cash money."

The report said twenty thousand. Which might mean that Lopez got off not because one of the arresting officers made a mistake, but because he knew the cops hadn't turned in all of the cash. And now he sat here grinning at her and there wasn't one thing she could say to get rid of that smug expression. Did

Riordan's Raiders use the cash as buy money, or did some of it find its way into a cop's pocket? Johnny wasn't there when the busts went down.

Marti wrote $250,000? large enough for Lopez to see, then put her notebook away. Let him wonder if that was why she came. "Thanks. I think you might have told me what I need to know."

Lopez stopped grinning. "This lady who brought my kid, she says she can help my old lady. That true?"

"She got your kid here within twenty-four hours, didn't she?"

Lopez thought about that for a minute and nodded his head. "Yeah." He looked down at the tattoo. "Damn, but I hate owing a cop. You know, Officer, Ma'am, the bust you might really be interested in happened about a year before the one you're asking about."

"Why would I be interested in something that far back?"

"Hell if I know, but since you asked me about Munoz, when he walked on this raid, someone said 'Hell, he walked a year ago, too.' Next thing you know, Munoz is dead."

And Johnny was, too. Was Munoz the snitch Johnny was going to see that night?

"Who said?" Marti asked.

Lopez shrugged. "It was just talk, you know. But talk gets around. Sometimes the wrong person hears."

Before they were out of the jail, Vik said, "We checked Munoz's arrest records. There wasn't anything to link him with Johnny, or Cantor, or DaVon."

"I know." There was just the word Johnny had been humming, chicomuno.

"Now we'll have to go back and look for an arrest about a year before the Lopez bust." Vik didn't sound so eager anymore. "What about the money? It wasn't on the report."

"They must have kept it for buy money. I don't know." A few weeks ago, she would not have believed Johnny would do anything that didn't follow department guidelines. Now she didn't know how much he would accept or overlook, or how far he would go to keep drugs off the streets. Johnny and his sister had argued so often that Marti hadn't realized how much her disappearance must have affected him.

"Did you know about any of this before now?" Vik asked.

"No," Marti admitted. "Riordan really kept a tight rein on his men. I never even heard a rumor. Of course, there were only about fifty narcs then. Everyone joked that there was so little action on the street that Crosby didn't have any reason to recruit. Riordan was able to keep his operation manageable and self-contained."

That was why Johnny said nothing. That's why the odor of sweat was so strong when he came home. Even now it was difficult for Marti to make the leap from the street buys and busts she thought Johnny was doing to the scope of the operation he was actually involved in.

"Think Riordan kept all of his men honest?" Vik asked.

"I think he would have to have maintained his integrity to foster their loyalty. Johnny didn't like him, but he did respect him."

Vik didn't question Johnny's integrity. Neither did Marti. She knew him well enough to be certain of that. But did he know something? Had someone in the department profited from these raids?

"We're going to have to talk to some more cops," Marti said. "And maybe it's time to talk with Lieutenant Dirkowitz again."

By the time she got home, Marti had a headache and an upset stomach. She took three Tylenol and half a dozen Mylanta tabs and went upstairs, intending to call Leotha when she got to her room. Instead, she took out Johnny's deck of cards. The throbbing in her forehead increased as she turned the cards over again. What secrets were lost to her? Was Chico the snitch, or was it Fayesta or Manuelito? They hadn't been able to find Fayesta last night. Was he avoiding them?

24

Monday morning, Marti and Vik met with a male uniform named Jack Kelly in a Kentucky Fried Chicken parking lot on the south side of Chicago. Kelly worked third shift and had agreed to meet with them on his way home. Marti remembered him as a young cop a couple of years out of the Academy. The cowlick was still there, but the toothy smile had been replaced by a tight-lipped nod and a wary, streetwise look.

Marti made the introductions. "I need to know about a drug raid you were in on about four years ago."

"Chico Munoz," Kelly said, after she explained. "A real piece of . . . garbage. I had a lot of respect for your husband, ma'am. Damned shame the way he went down. But when it came to snitches, he could sure pick 'em."

Vik sucked his teeth. Marti looked at him, daring him to offer his opinion of her snitches, which was similar.

"Damnedest thing, though," Kelly said. "They always came through for him."

"And Chico?"

"Chico the Weasel. Skinny little runt. He even looked like a weasel. After four years, the only thing I can tell you about this bust is that Chico was there when we went in. He didn't make it out in time. Johnny saw to it that he walked, but he was there."

"Anything different about the bust?" Marti asked.

"No, the usual. I'm sorry if this is important. I'd like to help you if I can, but I've thought about it since we talked last night, and I just can't think of anything at all."

"You were in on the Pittman Lopez raid, too."

"Yes ma'am."

"Johnny was involved in setting up both raids?"

"Yes."

"Other than Munoz was there anything similar or unusual about the raids?"

"No."

"I know you got a lot of cash and drugs in the Lopez raid."

Kelly was silent.

"And that you kept it for future operations."

There was no response.

"Can you tell me anything else about the Lopez bust?"

"Nothing you don't already know. It was a big one. Munoz was involved in setting it up. They found him a short time after your husband . . . but the Lopez raid wouldn't have had anything to do with Munoz dying. The weasel just OD'd. They all do sooner or later."

"Who's the dealer who got away?" Marti asked.

"Estlow. Slippery like an eel that one, and got nine lives."

"Anyone important get caught in either raid?"

"Middlemen. DEA can't even get to Estlow. Angelo Estlow. Angel. Man's got wings. Real escape artist. Never gets caught."

"Was Estlow the dealer involved with both raids?"

"Yep. And he got away both times. Just like Munoz. The man's becoming a legend in his own time. Out there somewhere right now giving us the finger. But they all make mistakes. We'll get him. The only good thing that came out of either raid didn't involve any of us, or Munoz or Lopez."

"What was that?"

"We busted a kid at the first raid, Hector Fuentes, printed him, released him on bail. A couple weeks later there was a shooting on the north side, near Peterson. Perp threw the gun in a Dumpster and guess what, it was traced back to Hector Fuentes. The prints we took after the raid matched prints found at a burglary where the gun had been stolen. And guess what, those prints also matched partials found on the weapon, and prints found on the bullets still in the chamber. Stupid, all of them. Stupid."

Marti was close to tears as they returned to Lincoln Prairie. This was like being lost in the woods and finding a path that didn't go anywhere.

"So," Vik said. "We've got Manuelito and Fayesta and now Lopez and Munoz . . . "

"And nothing," Marti said. "Nothing. Not one damned thing."

"Let's play it out," Vik said.

"Play what out?" Marti asked.

"Do you believe Johnny committed suicide?"

"No."

She wished she could close her eyes and block out the memory of Johnny sprawled in that car. She hadn't pictured the cemetery that way. Too many trees. There was no way he'd pick that place to die. She could hear herself telling that to Crosby or Riordan, or even Rivas.

A certainty filled her that she hadn't felt until now. "No, he didn't kill himself. I should have dealt with all of this a long time ago. So much time has passed now . . . "

"When you take Highway 51 in Wisconsin," Vik said, "you cross the Wisconsin River five times. It meanders all over the place. You drive down a straight road and keep going over it. But it begins somewhere, and it ends somewhere. So does this. Let's just go with it."

By mid-afternoon they knew that Hector Fuentes had been convicted at age eighteen of killing Francisco Santos, age thirteen. Johnny was not involved in that arrest. Fuentes was sentenced about six months before Johnny died. Marti could see no connection except that Johnny set up the raid where Fuentes was arrested and printed.

"Looks like Fuentes has been in and out of every major correctional institution in the state," Vik said. "Joliet, Pontiac, Statesville. Now he's at Menard."

"He's either got heavy gang connections or he's a real bad boy."

"Oops," Vik said. "He committed manslaughter while he was in Pontiac. He isn't ever coming home."

Denise Stevens had provided information on the minor. "The boy, Francisco Santos, was in the system, too," Marti said. "An abused child, with his mother at the time of his death."

Marti thought about Padgett. There was no evidence of physical abuse. Not with the mother. But in that environment, what else was happening to that child? Were they doing the right thing letting him stay there? She hoped Denise could provide enough support services to prevent another senseless death like Francisco Santos's. Denise was right. That did seem less likely if Padgett remained with Irene than if he took off on his own again.

25

It was almost four o'clock when Riordan's driver pulled into the parking lot at Meigs Field.

"Forty-two degrees," the driver said when Riordan got in the car. Here by the lake it would be cooler, but the streets and sidewalks were wet with melting snow and the sun so bright after months of overcast skies that the glare was almost blinding.

Riordan remained inside the car, drumming his fingers on the newspaper he'd tossed on the seat. He was being followed. He thought it had happened several times in the past few weeks, but on the way to Meigs Field he was certain. He had his driver radio in the license plate number. The make came back stolen, which was puzzling. He had assumed he was being watched by Internal Affairs, or by someone assigned to watch him by one of the other vice deputies. With two of his men dead and too many busts going sour, the vultures could be beginning to circle.

He drummed his fingers on the leather upholstery.

"Sir," the driver said. "They've got the car."

"Good. Who's in it?"

"They found it on the other side of Grant Park, Sir, a few blocks away. Empty."

Riordan cursed aloud. A stolen car. What if this wasn't one of his own?

Turning, he looked at the planes tied down near the runway, wondering which one was Crosby's. Dan had a new toy and couldn't wait to show it off. A boat, condos on Cape Cod and in Fort Lauderdale, a cabin on a lake in Wisconsin. More than Riordan would ever have. The insurance fraud business must be booming. Two hundred and fifty thousand would only go so far.

Crosby had no wives, no kids, no alimony, no college tuition. He got to keep all of his money for himself. It must be nice.

Crosby paced alongside the Cherokee Six. Where in the hell was Riordan? If he didn't come . . . A gust of wind made him lurch against the wing. Crosby moved away from the aircraft, admired the shiny blue paint, moved closer and ran his hand along the black stripes. Brand new, and all his. He couldn't wait until he could fly solo and take Joey with him. He couldn't even wait until Joey's birthday.

Crosby turned to see Riordan coming toward him.

"Hey, Joey, take a look!"

Crosby walked Riordan around the airplane. "Guess how high she gets. Go ahead, guess."

Riordan shrugged and shook his head, smiling as Crosby told him.

"You want to fly her, Joey? Just take lessons. Hey, I'll spring for the lessons. Come on. What do you say?"

"Someday, maybe."

"Here, come on, look inside."

"I told you, no flying. I like my airplanes big. Room for a hundred and twenty-seven passengers at least, not six including the pilot."

"Come on."

Inside, Crosby sat at the controls. "See this, Joey?" He pointed to a circular instrument in the center of the panel. "VOR. High range navigational radio. And the round thing in the upper left corner there, with the red, green, and white arcs—air speed indicator. And this, guess what Joey, this baby is the LORAN—real important, tells you how to get to the airport." Crosby laughed.

"And flying, Joey, it's incredible. This is the real thing, like the Wright Brothers. Nothing up there but you and the clouds and the sky and the wind. One mistake, one, and boom." He snapped his fingers. "You're dead, man. You are dead."

Crosby nudged Riordan's thigh. "Bet you didn't think I'd ever do anything like this, did you?"

"I didn't think you'd take up sailing, either. You handling that boat by yourself yet?"

"This summer, Joey. My instructor says I'm almost ready to solo. Just me and you, kid. Just me and you. Nothing else like sailing, except flying."

"What's next?"

"Who knows, Joey. Who knows? Hot air balloons, maybe. I've been thinking about that. Or alpine skiing." He leaned back, surveying the runway grid. "Hey, Joey, you want lessons, they're yours."

"Sure. I'll give it some thought. But I gotta get back now. I got work to do. I haven't been let out to pasture yet like you."

"This is a long way from Bridgeport, ain't it?"

"Right, Danny boy, it sure is."

As Riordan walked away, a gust of wind caught at his coat, blowing it open. Like wings, Crosby thought. When they were kids growing up together, Joey's dad was a homicide dick. His own father never made it past beat cop. Neither man ever left Deering District in Bridgeport. Look at what their sons had become: vice deputy. All this talk of Joey being in line to become superintendent; with the bad luck he'd been having lately, there didn't seem to be much chance of that.

The door opened suddenly. Crosby reached for his gun.

"Hey, Chief. It's just me," his flight instructor said. "Didn't mean to startle you. You cops sure are jumpy."

"I'm not a cop anymore."

"The hell you aren't."

The young man with blond hair laughed and climbed in.

"Here. Let me." Crosby rested one hand on his instructor's leg as he reached across him to pull the door shut.

26

Marti drove back to the city to see Rachel on Monday night. Having made the trip once today, she wasn't sure why she was returning. She had been putting it off because she didn't know how much she wanted to tell Rachel, or whether she should tell her anything at all.

They went to the kitchen, a small room with white walls and diagonal black and white tiles that made it look larger than it was. Fat red poppies seemed to jump from a canvas hung between two windows. They sat at a table with a lace table cloth and crystal salt and pepper shakers. Rachel poured tea from a black ceramic pot into fat red mugs.

"How're you doing?" Marti asked, but she could see. There were circles under Rachel's eyes, and her fawn slacks and beige blouse seemed to hang on her.

"It's time to start the tomatoes," Rachel said. "I have a place in the basement with special lights where Julian grew them until it was warm enough to put them outside. We'd have fresh tomatoes from June until October."

One of the dogs came in. Rachel stroked its head until it lay at her feet with a sigh.

"Are you doing anything?" Rachel asked. "Are you getting anywhere?"

Marti hesitated, thinking of what the lieutenant had said about a hysterical woman. She nodded. When she didn't offer anything else, Rachel said, "What can you tell me?"

"Nothing much. You're going to have to trust me."

"Trust you? That's cop talk for you don't trust me."

"I've been where you are," Marti said.

Rachel looked at her for a minute. "Yes, I forget. I think I'm the only woman this has ever happened to. But there are many of us, aren't there?" She pulled the dog onto her lap, speaking with her face against its fur.

"Julian and I never had much more than each other. There were no children. There was never enough time to be together. Never enough. We didn't go out often, just to family things, the synagogue. I don't do very much. The dogs. Shopping." Rachel smiled. "My mother wants me to come home. My father wants me to work in one of his stores like I did when I was a teenager. I used to know how to help keep the books, but now there are so many stores, and accountants and lawyers. And I'm not daddy's little girl anymore. I don't want to be anyone's little girl ever again." She looked around the room. "That, and being a wife. There's not much else I know how to do."

Marti couldn't remember being like this. The children made too many demands. Momma bustled in every day and refused to allow her to mope. The only time she was alone was at night, and sometimes she was tired enough to sleep.

"What can you tell me?" Rachel asked. "Do *snitch* and *Lope* mean anything?"

Again Marti hesitated. "I'm working on it. Nothing seems to be . . . straightforward. So much time has passed. You'll have to be patient for a while."

"You sound discouraged," Rachel said. "Look, I know you don't want to tell me anything. You're a cop, that's natural. But maybe there's some way I can help."

Marti shook her head. It seemed as if everything led to a dead end. But she wasn't going to give up.

"I'm going through all of his things, Marti. His old notebooks, everything."

"That's good."

"I'm going to help you," Rachel said. "I have to help you."

"You already have," Marti told her. "Just be patient. It gets better. It really does get better. And please find something to do. You worry me."

Rachel hugged her. Without understanding why, Marti felt comforted.

27

Monday night Diablo returned to Meigs Field, parking in an underground garage and walking through Grant Park, switchblade ready. Diablo hurried past the Field Museum, zigzagged across Lake Shore Drive, then walked quickly to the road that led to the chain link fence surrounding the airfield. There were no guards.

Diablo climbed over the fence, crouched down, and approached Crosby's airplane. This place was nothing like O'Hare. Everything shut down at ten o'clock.

Diablo checked the lock on the door, tried keys until one fit but wouldn't turn, and played with that one and a file until the grooves matched close enough and the door opened.

The airplane was facing the round dome of the planetarium. Inside, six seats were crowded together. The whole front was nothing but clocks and dials, needles and switches. Diablo sat in the pilot's seat, put on the headset, tried to imagine what it would be like to fly. Wind and sky and freedom, like a bird. Impossible to imagine after years in a jail cell.

But that time had not been wasted. At first it was enough to have killed MacAlister. But then, sitting in that cell, Diablo had begun to think of others who also deserved to die. Crosby, Riordan, Murphy, Jamison . . . the list was long and there was plenty of time.

In jail there was so much to learn, so many ways to kill. Diablo liked making bombs because it required so much skill. Fires seemed the most fun.

Diablo took off the headset and looked up at the sky, then out at the lake. Too bad there was no way to fly in this. The pilot would soon be dead. Riordan had come here today, met Crosby. Maybe Riordan would come back, fly in this with Crosby, maybe not. It didn't matter. There was another plan for Riordan. Diablo smiled. Hell of a lot easier to get at this than to get at Riordan's car. And with this place locked up all night, and no security guard, plenty of time to get this bird ready to fly. Which instrument should the bomb be rigged to? Maybe there was a manual somewhere.

Marti was at her desk Tuesday morning going through some routine reports when DaVon's partner, Jim Bauer, came in.

"Jim!" He looked gaunt. There were dark circles under his eyes, as if he hadn't got much sleep lately. "Are you all right?"

He shrugged and sat down. Marti brought him some coffee. "How's it going?"

"I'm all right. I'm getting ready to go back to work. I just needed some time to myself."

"Would you like to go someplace and talk?"

"No. No, this is fine. I had a hard time finding the place. Drove past twice on forty-one. I, um, DaVon was talking a lot about Johnny before he died."

Marti felt queasy. "Something I should know?"

"Just . . . the job. But he was so . . . he was drinking . . . more than I'd ever seen him drink before. He, um, he just kept talking about Johnny, about old times, about when they rode together. It was like he couldn't get Johnny off his mind." He gulped at the coffee. "This probably isn't helping you. I'm sorry. DaVon just kept remembering all of these stories about when they rode together. He told them to me over and over. I don't know why I came here. I can't tell you anything you don't know. I just needed to say hello, touch base, you know."

Marti nodded. She didn't understand what Jim was trying to tell her, but she did understand his loss.

"It could have been me instead of DaVon. I just happened to be on the other side of the ram."

"DaVon was the only one who got shot."

"Yeah. Guy who did it was just a kid. Nineteen. He panicked. We nailed him. The others, they had their hands up. Thank God there were only four of them and we kept our heads and only the kid got killed. Everything was up for grabs when that gun went off. If there had been women in there, or children . . . " He shuddered. "You never know what the hell's waiting for you when that door goes down."

"You sure you're ready to go back?"

His laugh was nervous. "I think I'm going to take it slow. And I might not go through any more doors, but you know how it is— once a cop . . . "

"Yes," Marti said. "I know."

"How's things with you?"

"I've been doing a little investigating on my own into Johnny's death."

"I know. Jamison told me. She said you wanted to see me. But I don't think I can be of any help."

Without going into detail, Marti gave him a quick overview.

"DaVon did mention a Fayesta."

"He did? What did he say?"

Jim shook his head. "Nothing coherent. He was drunk."

"When?"

"Oh, I don't know. Maybe the week before he died. He talked about a lot of other people, too. Not anything that made any sense."

"What was he talking about when he mentioned Fayesta?"

Jim thought for a minute, then laughed. "Either the beach, or someone named Sanders. I'm not sure which. He liked to sit by the lake and drink. So it could have been either."

Or Santos, maybe. Francisco Santos.

After Jim left, Marti put in a call to Leotha. She needed more information.

That afternoon, Marti and Vik drove to the west side of Chicago, the Pilson area, about twelve blocks from where Marti grew up. The house where Francisco Santos's mother lived at the time of his death had burned down. They were going to see Santos's grandmother, the next address that Denise had tracked down for them. It turned out to be a small, one-story house, with soft asbestos shingles manufactured in the fifties. Three young children played on a wooden porch that was missing parts of the railing. Despite the cold, the children wore light jackets and didn't have on hats or mittens.

Vik grumbled under his breath. "I hate it when they don't have warm clothes to wear. Why do people have children if this is the way they take care of them?"

"This is the grandmother's house," Marti said.

"That doesn't make any difference."

Vik got out first, slammed the car door, and stomped up five sagging steps, muttering to himself. Marti knew he was thinking as much about Padgett as he was about the children on the porch.

A frail, elderly woman opened the door. She was wearing rubber thongs and a misshapen cardigan. Her yellow-white hair was pulled into a neat bun at the nape of her neck. She cautioned the children in Spanish to stay on the porch away from the street, to duck down if they saw a car drive along slowly, and to come inside if they saw anyone who belonged to a gang. She called the youngest to her, put her hands on his ears, and sent him back with a quick hug. Apparently he wasn't too cold to stay out.

Marti noted with relief that the child went to his grandmother without hesitation and that the children were clean.

"This might go better in Spanish," Vik said to Marti. "You want to interpret?"

"I'd just as soon keep the advantage and let her try it in English first."

The living room was furnished with two cots and a sagging couch. An electric heater kept the room warm. The place was clean—no garbage, no piles of dirty clothes, no roaches—but it was easy to see that the old woman was having a hard time.

"We've come to ask you about Francisco," Marti said.

"After all of this time? It has been a long time since anyone cared."

Marti sat on the edge of the sofa and gripped her hands together. "Can you tell us what happened one more time?"

"Francisco, he is thirteen. He is with his mother, my daughter. He is not such a good boy, but he tries. They are not living here. They are living near where he is killed. I do not know why he goes into the street that night. Probably to beg. They tell me when the police go to the house, there is no food, that the children are hungry."

Tears rolled down the old woman's face and she wiped them with the back of her hand. "Francisco does not need our tears now. He is with God."

"Had he lived there long?" Marti asked.

"For a few months. His mother does not stay any place very long."

"It happened after midnight. Why would he have been out that late? There were no stores open then, just a few bars."

The old woman looked down, fingering the edge of the sweater. "He was hungry. I do not know. He had been told not to beg."

When Marti returned to the car, Vik got in beside her and pounded his fist into the palm of his hand.

Marti drove a short distance and stopped in front of a small store with children's clothing hanging in the windows.

"I'm no good at sizes," Vik said.

"I am."

Together they picked out three warm coats and hats and mittens to match. Then they went to the grocery store and bought beans and rice, fruit and milk and orange juice and eggs. They split the cost.

"We'll talk to Denise," Marti said. "There's probably a way to get somebody in there to do a few things for the old lady without being too intrusive. The old woman just needs a little help. You can see that she loves them."

When Marti checked her answering machine before driving back to Lincoln Prairie, Manuelito had called. Fayesta came to his house last Friday night, afraid because someone was after him. He left Saturday morning and Manuelito had not heard from him or been able to reach him since. Fayesta must be dead, Manuelito said, and it was his fault. When Marti called Manuelito back, she got his machine and left a message that she hoped was reassuring.

Fayesta lived in a better neighborhood than Marti expected. Even so, gang symbols painted on brick walls staked out territories. It was after dark by the time Vik and Marti got there. The landlord lived on the premises and unlocked the door to an apartment on the second floor, rear.

"Ain't see him since the weekend," he said, rubbing a stubble of beard. "Just close the door when you're done. It'll lock."

The apartment was small. Vik took the kitchen and Marti the bedroom. The breasts weren't real. Fayesta had a drawer filled with padded bras in various sizes. The bottom drawer of the nightstand was filled with photographs. Most seemed to be of Fayesta's family, although Marti didn't recognize Fayesta in any of those. The recent photos were pornographic and there were multiple copies.

"Maybe he passes out pictures of himself to prospective clients," Vik said. "Maybe he just likes looking at himself this way. I think we should keep one set. Just in case. Who knows, we might be looking at him with his killer."

There was nothing else in the apartment that seemed important.

"Fayesta might get along pretty well with Joanna," Vik said. "Vitamins, tofu, bean sprouts, the whole nine yards. And lots of prescriptions, not Valium or sleeping pills—antibiotics and Zantac, ulcers maybe. Job-related stress."

Marti thought of the photographs. A lot of them were of three little girls and two little boys. She wondered which one of them was Fayesta.

When they went back outside Marti realized just how dark it was. Several streetlights were out. As they stood in the doorway, a car drove past. "Gang territory," Marti said, stepping back.

They had parked almost a block away. Most of the cars that had prevented their parking closer were gone. Marti turned up her collar to block the wind.

"Damn but it's cold," Vik said.

They were several blocks from a main street and there was no traffic here. Out of habit, Marti said, "Two men on foot, just down the street to the right."

The men went into a doorway and Vik and Marti drew their weapons. Marti kept hers pointed down, with her finger away from the trigger. The doorway was empty when they reached it. The weather seemed to be keeping most folks inside. They stopped before crossing an alley, checking first.

"No lights there either," Vik said.

"They shoot them out."

Metal rattled, and a cat yowled.

Marti jumped. "Damn." Her heart was pounding. She holstered her gun.

Two blocks away, a car turned the corner.

"Could be the same one that just went past," Marti said. "If the headlights go out, take cover."

The car approached them with its brights on. When the lights went out, Marti hit the ground rolling. The gunshot was like an explosion. Before she could react, the car sped away.

"You okay, Jessenovik?"

"Just fine," Vik said. "I get shot at every other day. Was this just a random drive-by?"

"I'm not sure," Marti admitted.

"Did you see the plates?"

"Looked like PD10 . . . "

"No," Vik disagreed. "BG."

Crosby pulled over six blocks from where Fayesta lived. The pain in his chest was bad. He saw little explosions of light in front of his eyes. Gasping, he tried to take deep breaths, but it hurt. He panted instead until the pain subsided. He was okay now. It was just stress.

What was MacAlister's wife doing there? He knew how much MacAlister had found out, but what did she know? MacAlister couldn't have told her. She wouldn't have waited all of this time to do something about it. And who was this Fayesta? He had driven past that building for three days, trying to make up his mind whether to go in or not. Now that woman had beat him to it. What had she found there?

He shouldn't have shot at her. He should have kept going. Had she had enough time to see the plate before he blinded her with the brights? Another stupid mistake. He needed a plan. Or Estlow. Yes, he'd let Estlow handle this. That was what he should do.

Marti sought out the comfort of the kitchen when she got home, grateful for warm yellow walls and the dim circle of light from the lamp. She hadn't eaten anything since lunch and wasn't hungry, but she fixed a cup of chamomile tea.

Sharon came downstairs while Marti was sitting in the rocking chari near the window, looking out at the darkness. Was it just a random drive-by shooting, or had she placed them in danger? How could anyone know she would be at Fayesta's apartment?

Sharon pulled up a chair beside her.

"You're in awfully late. It's almost morning. Are you working a new case?"

Marti shook her head.

Sharon remained beside her, and when their silence became comfortable, Marti said, "I don't talk much about the job."

"No."

"Do you wonder about what I do?"

"Of course."

"Do you want to know?"

"I'm not sure."

"I see things sometimes . . . If anyone had told me beforehand, I'd be doing something else."

"Some jobs, they have these debriefing sessions."

"We have department shrinks, but being a woman . . . you have to be careful. They might say we can't handle the job." She thought about Dirkowitz's comment, about her and Vik getting emotionally involved. At least some people thought it was okay.

"Do you get harassed much?" Sharon asked.

"Not anymore. Not that there aren't guys out there who think we're a joke."

"How do you keep them in line?"

"Depends. Sometimes you confront them, sometimes you ignore them. Most of the time I just do my job."

"Don't you get mad? You put your life on the line, same as they do. You're always so calm about most things. You're much better at accepting people the way they are than I ever was."

Marti took a sip of tea. It was still warm. "You change the things you can. The rest will just get you frustrated."

"Do you want to talk with me about the job, with anyone?"

"I don't know. Johnny and I didn't talk much about it."

"You didn't? I always thought you talked about everything."

"No. And, I'm not sure why not. I always thought we needed this little oasis where things were normal. I thought we didn't want the things we had to deal with to intrude. Now I'm not so sure. Not talking about it was easier. There are times I would have cried . . . it was important to me that Johnny always thought I was strong. I didn't want to be this weeping, whining woman. Momma's strong. I'm like her. There were times when she'd come home from cleaning those trains and I knew someone had given her a hard time, but she never said a word. I wanted to be like that, strong."

"I know. There are things I never tell a man. Too risky."

Marti felt that way, too. But what would she have been risking? Johnny knew everything else about her, and she knew just about everything about him. Except for 'Nam. Except for the job. Except for what caused them both the most pain. They had kept most of their pain and their anger to themselves.

She and Johnny were supposed to be partners. When had they stopped talking about the job? When the excitement wore off and the teduim set in? When the violence became so repetitious that it began grinding them down?

There were nights when she wanted to scream with the pain of seeing a child who had been tortured to death. Instead, she went home and hugged her own children, and when Johnny came home, fixed his dinner and maybe danced with him. It felt so good, being in his arms. She had clung to him, forcing the memory of those bruised and battered little bodies to go away, and had headaches for two days afterward, or woke up sweating and unable to sleep. And Johnny, the only person she was close to who could have understood, never asked any questions, never told her when he was in pain.

How much had it cost them both to remain silent? Theo seemed to remember a man who had never spoken at all. Did Theo sense all that they were holding back? Did Joanna?

What else had Johnny kept from her? How much pain and anger and confusion he must have hidden from her over the years, having nightmares instead, or refusing to go to places like Devil's Lake and the Dells. Was he that quiet because he was afraid of what he would say if he started talking? Why couldn't he talk to her? Why couldn't he trust her?

30

Marti and Vik took Wednesday off to go to Chester, Illinois. It was a six and a half hour drive on Interstate 55, so they left at five in the morning. Menard was one of the oldest penal institutions in the state, and had been built along the banks of the Mississippi.

Marti had spoken with the warden. Fuentes was doing well at Menard. To get there he had fought, joined gangs, used drugs, and killed another inmate, and now he'd be eligible for parole in twenty-eight years.

"A bad one," Vik said. "The kind you're glad to see get locked up. If he hadn't got caught for killing that kid, I bet he'd be somebody's hit man."

Visitors parking consisted of the mud and snow along the perimeter of the lot. Marti opted for employees parking. Vik flipped down the visor and attached their Lincoln Prairie Police identification.

Inside, the place reminded Marti of a Cagney movie. By the time they walked through two sets of heavy iron bars and watched as the guard locked them with a huge key, Marti was so twitchy she was almost ready to leave.

The visitors room consisted of chairs, tables, vending machines, and dingy walls. Marti felt hot and confined. Vik loosened his tie. Fuentes was short and stocky, with a round, pudgy face. Dark circles under his eyes and sluggish movements indicated that he was on medication. He was twenty-two years old and looked fifteen.

"Yeah, you wan' me? Wha' you wan'?"

Vik glanced at Marti and said, "We want to talk with you about that night in Chicago when the boy died."

"Yeah. I bet you do." He didn't sound hostile, just drowsy. "Wha' you wan' now? You wan' me to tell you I did it?"

"Did you?" Vik asked.

"I kill one man in here." He held up one finger. "No boy."

"Why did you say that you did?"

"You lie. All of you. You lie." He spoke with resignation. The anger, the temper, whatever had driven him to get into so much trouble seemed to be gone.

"Look, son," Vik said, speaking softly as he leaned forward and looked Fuentes in the eye. "I'm not a Chicago cop. I just want you to tell me what happened. I can't promise that it'll help you. But I'd sure appreciate knowing."

That seemed to calm Fuentes. "I'm there when they bust Lopez. I have a gun. We all have a gun. There are many guns, money, drugs. The cops take it all. The cops take the guns. A week later I am sleeping and they bust in the door and arrest me. I do not speak much English then. I do not understand English very good. The man comes and speaks to me in Spanish. I tell him what happens, they write it down, I sign. Then they say it says that I kill him."

"Did you bring a gun there?"

"The gun that kills the kid? I take one while I am stealing. If it was the gun that killed him, it was mine. It was there. They took it."

"How much money?" Vik asked.

"Fifty grand, maybe."

"And drugs?"

Fuentes smiled. "Mucho crack. Enough to stay high for a lifetime."

"Why were you there?"

"I was there with . . . friends. I have nothing to do with drugs."

"You had already committed at least one burglary. That's how you got the gun."

"That's not like killing no one, man."

"Did you kill him?"

"What difference does it make now? I never get out of here."

When Marti spoke with Leotha the day before, she agreed to stop by with Vik on their way back from Menard. Leotha eyed Vik for a minute when they arrived. "So this is your partner." She invited them into the kitchen where she set out slices of turkey, thick slices of rye bread, and a tureen of homemade vegetable soup. They sat at a glass and rattan table and made sandwiches.

"How was your trip to the big house?" Leotha asked. "I arrested Fuentes's sister once. She has priors going back years before he came here."

Marti thought about the doors clanging shut behind her and shuddered. She let Vik do the talking.

"Would his interpreter have lied?" Vik said.

"Maybe. If he didn't like Latinos, or drug dealers, or gang members, or if he was in a bad mood, or there was a full moon . . . ."

"Or if he got paid," Vik said.

"Maybe. And not necessarily in currency. Sometimes the right favor can take you a long way. Depends on your agenda." Leotha popped open a beer. "I suppose things like that don't happen in Lincoln Prairie."

"I suppose anything's possible," Vik said, to Marti's surprise. "But I don't think so." He picked up a knife and spread a thick layer of mustard. "I couldn't work here. Everything's too big."

Marti told Leotha about the bar blowing up.

"And you don't miss the action, Marti?" Leotha said. "A few months of that would be a great vacation, but I'm not sure I could make it a permanent lifestyle."

"I feel like a real cop now," Marti said. "I solve cases, I don't just get lucky. When I get home at night I feel like I've done what I'm trained to do, what I do best, and I've done it well. Sometimes I get frustrated, but not like I did here."

Leotha cleared the table and got out a pack of cigarettes. "The pace would be too slow for me, but since you've got all this time on your hands, why don't you tell me what else has been happening."

Marti looked at Vik. He nodded.

She told Leotha what she knew. "What about Estlow? His name keeps coming up."

"That's because he's controlling our Mexican supply. We want him, the DEA wants him. But the man has nine lives. He just keeps getting away. It's gotten to be like a game. We win some, he wins some. We lose, he loses. We'll get him sooner or later. Estlow doesn't care any more about a cop going down than he cares about one of his own men going down. Estlow cares about money, about drugs, same as us. We just like to keep our body count at zero, while someone else's life doesn't mean shit to him.

"The way I see it, MacAlister, we've got a dead kid and a guy doing time for it who may or may not be guilty. We've got three cops—Riordan, Crosby, and Murphy—who may or may not have walked out of a raid with a lot of money and a lot of cocaine. And we have Cantor, DaVon, and Johnny, also deceased."

Marti thought about getting shot at the night before and decided not to mention it. She got gooseflesh and rubbed her arms. "Put like that . . ."

"And that's how I think we should put it, just to keep things in perspective. Crosby is the only one who is retired and prospering. If anyone has made out since this happened, it's Crosby and Riordan, because Crosby put him into his job. Assuming there was money and drugs, I think the key questions are: How much was there, who got it, and what did they do with it."

"I think Fuentes might be the key," Marti said. "The money and the drugs would have been less important to Johnny than making the busts. If Fuentes got set up, that might have bothered him, if only because the kid's arrest was the direct result of a raid he engineered."

"Damn," Leotha said. "Don't tell me it might be something that has nothing to do with Riordan or Crosby. I was hoping for a little routine corruption."

"The more we find out, the less we seem to know," Marti said.

"Just watch your back," Leotha said. "Someone's been following me. They had a key to this building. I almost caught them last night. And Riordan's really out to get me."

"We were shot at last night leaving Fayesta's apartment," Marti said. "I don't know if it's something to worry about."

"My aunt lives six blocks from there. It used to be a nice neighborhood, but the gang activity has really escalated in the past two years."

Marti thought of her "gingerbread house" in Lincoln Prairie and Sharon and their kids safe inside, and wondered how safe all of them were. She had been asking people questions. Cantor and DaVon had done that and they were dead. Fayesta was missing. Marti felt her skin prickle. "Someone walking on your grave," Momma would say.

When they finished their meal, Leotha made some calls. "Fuentes's brother lives about an hour from here. His sister lives a little closer. The sister's been busted a couple times since the last time I saw her, for intent to deliver a controlled substance—small quantities, but enough to do a little time in Cook County Jail. And Hector wasn't as innocent as he says. For someone who'd only been in this country for five months he had one hell of a juvenile record—burglaries, theft, but no battery or weapons charges. Want to go meet his relatives?"

They agreed that Marti and Leotha would do the talking this time while Vik waited in the car, since cops didn't usually travel in threes. Marti thought of the drive-by last night and felt more than a little relieved to have Vik watching outside.

31

Later that night Marti, Vik, and Leotha took the Eisenhower to Hillside, a small community far enough from the city limits to let the residents forget about gangs and drugs and violence. Newer ranches and trilevels spread out on double lots alongside older and smaller wood frames and brick bungalows. The streets were lined with leafless trees. Small patches of winter-brown grass amid mounds of snow were minute reminders that winter would come to an end.

"Turn left at the corner," Leotha directed.

The sister's address turned out to be one of the newer brick ranches. A BMW was parked in front of a closed garage.

"Not bad for someone with no known source of income," Leotha said.

She alternately rang the bell and waited for ten minutes before a petite Hispanic woman answered the door.

"What do you want?" the woman asked, yawning and rubbing her eyes. "What is it now? I have done nothing. Nothing. Why can't you leave me alone?"

The woman seemed both old and young, her face set in a scowl that had etched lines into the corners of her eyes and mouth. There was a haggardness about her, as if she were ill. Marti guessed her age as around thirty-five.

"Hi, Juanita," Leotha said. "I'd just like to ask you a few questions."

"Questions. Always it is questions. What is it now?"

"It's about your brother, Hector."

"Oh my God." Juanita turned pale and sagged against the door. "Oh my God, he is dead." She crossed herself and said in Spanish,

"I will take it to my grave that they killed him."

Marti wondered what she was using. Whatever it was, she needed a fix.

"Perhaps we should go inside," Leotha sugested. They walked through a living room decorated in blue and mauve to a kitchen with the same color scheme.

"Those bastards. He does nothing and they lock him up. They treat him like an animal. They rape him, they make a little girl of him and now they kill him. Who does this? Who does this to my brother? The guards or those bastards he is locked up with?"

Juanita folded her arms and paced. Marti and Leotha sat on stools at a table in the center of the room.

"He's not dead," Leotha said.

"Then what? You come to tell me he is in more trouble, that he killed someone again? Dear God, what more can happen to him? What has he done now?"

"Nothing that I know of," Leotha said.

"Then why are you here?" Juanita shouted.

"We're taking another look at his case," Leotha said calmly. "I just wanted to ask you a few questions."

"Oh. Hector is in prison all this time and now the cops want to ask me some questions. Maybe if you had asked a few more questions in the first place . . . "

"Did you live in the area where the boy was killed?"

"No! Goddammit, you already know that."

Juanita went to the window and leaned against it, looking out. "We were in Pilson then. I came here first, then sent for my family." Her pensiveness sounded as intense now as her anger had been a moment ago.

"I brought Hector here. And for what? My brother speaks very little English. He is not quick to learn, like I am. The interpreter did not say what Hector told him—that he knew nothing. He said Hector confessed. What my brother said in Spanish was not recorded—only what the interpreter repeated in English. My brother nodded his head, said *si*. He thought they both said the same thing. Because there was this—confession—there was nothing we could do."

"How much do you remember about what Hector did the day the young boy died?" Leotha asked.

"I remember that Hector was with me. I told them that. They did not believe me."

Since Juanita already had a record, Marti wasn't surprised.

"Where were you that day?"

"At my place. I used to cook for him. He drank too much wine and slept on the couch. That is where the police found him the next morning."

Juanita started pacing again, gesturing with her hands as she spoke. "They said that the gun was his, that he stole it. He told them in Spanish that they had taken the gun already, in a drug raid. I repeated it in English. They laughed and said, 'Sure, right.' They did not believe him."

She stopped suddenly and lowered her voice. "You are cops, you know this. There is nothing to do now but watch him die a little more each day in that jail. There were no appeals, nothing."

"Why was he at Pittman Lopez's place?"

"Why do you ask me that?" Her anger flared again. "He went because I sent him there. It was an errand, to get something I had forgotten. Hector has nothing to do with drugs. He never had nothing to do with drugs, he is a good boy. He never did any of the things they accuse him of. He is innocent. Hector, he does nothing wrong. In court Hector's lawyer tried to say it was my fault, that I brought him here to steal, to sell drugs. That is why they do not believe what I say. That is why they do not believe what Hector tells them, that he did not kill that boy."

Leotha stood up. "Well, your story certainly hasn't changed. I'll be in touch if I need anything else."

"You said there is something new."

"I said we're taking another look at his case."

"Liars!" Juanita said. "Always you lie." Then, "There will not be more trouble for him?"

"No," Leotha said. "Sounds like it would just be a waste of my time. There won't be more trouble."

Juanita moved toward the door, eager to get them out. On the way back to the car Marti said, "A little erratic, isn't she?"

"Drug addict," Leotha said. "And I think we woke her up. Give her another ten minutes to get high and she might be a different person."

Marti could see that Leotha was charged with the thrill of pursuit, as Johnny used to call it.

Victor Fuentes, Hector's brother, lived in Oak Lawn.

"Suburbia, USA," Leotha said as they parked near a trilevel house with a basketball hoop alongside the driveway. "We do like our BMWs. His occupation is a little vague—investment counselor, real estate agent, he buys and sells vintage cars. Squeaky clean. The only thing we've got on him is few speeding tickets. Makes you wonder."

Victor was in the garage now, poking around the engine of a shiny old roadster.

"Yes? What do you want? I don't need cops here. Make it fast."

He already knew they were cops. Was it that obvious, or had Juanita called him?

"Hector, always it is Hector. Or Juanita. As if I am responsible for what either of them does."

Victor spoke with only a trace of an accent. He was about five seven, give or take half an inch, and muscular with the beginnings of a paunch. Dark curly hair framed his round face. He was a few years younger than his sister.

"We wanted to ask you a few questions about Hector."

"Why? What good will that do now? Why didn't you ask any questions when you arrested him? Why didn't you care what his family said then? We tried to tell you he is innocent. Instead you send him away and then he does get into trouble. Don't come here now and ask me anything. He's killed someone now. He will never get out of that place."

A cordless phone chirped. "Yes," he said, then listened. "No. Call me back."

"This killed my father and almost killed my mother. They came here because this is a land of opportunity. Instead you take their youngest child and make a killer of him. It broke their hearts. Go away."

Vik was fidgety as Marti filled him in.

"What are the odds that this kid was set up?" he asked.

"Deliberately?" Leotha asked. "Odds are slim. But for the hell of it? Maybe. Look at it this way, the kid was already in trouble. With a sister like that leading the way, he wasn't going to get any better."

"Hell of a thing for the family, though," Vik said.

Leotha shrugged. "So he killed some con at twenty-one. Who knows, if he was on the street instead, he might have killed one of us even sooner. These kids don't go straight, Vik. They don't get rehabilitated. They get worse. And one day, they die. Their families can weep and moan and what if, but I see the end result everyday. If there is any tragedy here, it's that the sister got started long before he did and she pulled him right in, before he had a chance to stay straight. All that anger big sister's pushing off on us? She's just pissed because he's in there and not out here to aid and abet her. Fuentes didn't even speak English back then. Why do you think he went to Lopez's place? To pick up something she forgot? Don't be stupid. He was either delivering something or making a buy. Juanita was selling to school kids to support her habit. Do you think she gave a damn about her baby brother?"

32

Juanita was sitting in her living room with the lights out waiting for Estlow when he arrived a little after midnight. She opened the door with the chain on and made sure he was alone, then let him in.

She put her arms around him, kissing him before he could take off his coat. "Everything okay? I was getting worried."

"Everything's fine, baby. You're fine, too." He smiled and took a packet out of his pocket. "See, I bring you the finest girl in town."

Juanita took the bag of cocaine, weighing it in her hand. There was enough for two, three days maybe. "You sure you weren't followed? What if you got caught while you were carrying this?"

"Come on baby, I told you. They can't touch me, not Angel."

Juanita hung up his coat. For as long as she could remember, Estlow had too much confidence. For as long as she could remember, he had been lucky. He always got away. She didn't believe in luck. None of Estlow's luck had rubbed off on her. Nothing had been lucky for Hector.

"You've got to be careful. Please."

"No. You're the one who's got to be careful, baby. You can't fuck up anymore. Everything you want, everything you need, I give you, and still you get into trouble and get your ass locked up in jail. Always, when it is good, you do something to screw things up."

Juanita blew him a kiss. "I love you, too, baby. And I'm cool now. Everything's cool."

She followed him into the kitchen, leaning against the sink and watching as he opened the refrigerator door. He was so tall and broad-shouldered, strong. And not pretty. A rugged face, with small acne scars. Dark eyes. Eyes that missed nothing, forgot nothing.

He turned to her with a can of Pepsi in his hand. She smiled, seeing the pleasure in his eyes as he looked at her.

"So, 'Nita, if everything is so cool, why are the cops here?"

"They say there is new information about Hector."

"Hector, Hector. Give it up, 'Nita. Some men are weak."

"He wanted to be like you."

"So? He is not."

Sometimes, when he talked like that, it made her mad. Tonight she stroked the plastic-wrapped packet and put it into the freezer. Everything was cool.

"So, Sergeant Jamison was here. What did you tell her?"

"What I tell them all, that Hector is innocent."

"That is all?"

"What else is there to tell? Who talks to cops?" Had she said more than she should have? It was such a surprise, seeing them there when she went to the door.

"And the other one? Her partner?"

"Nothing."

Estlow drained the can and came over to her. She put her lips to his, tasting the soda.

"You have time to stay for a few hours, or are you leaving?"

Estlow laughed. It was a laugh deep with the joy of being alive. It reminded her that Hector would never laugh again. She turned her face from him.

"Hey, baby. It's me, your angel."

"You only brought enough for a couple of days."

"More and you might try to sell it."

"Maybe you shouldn't leave me alone."

He laughed again. "There is too much work to be done."

"They got everything out of that house in time?"

"Not only was the place clean when the cops came, we had a mommy inside with two little babies to be frightened and scream when they broke down the door."

"And you, you were out of there again, just in time?"

"Just in time." He touched her hair, pressed the pulse in her throat, caressed her breasts. "Crosby thinks that he tells us just enough to keep us nipping at Riordan's heels. But once he gives me the time and place of the raid, I have a safe house until they come. I bring everything there. Crosby is much more useful than he knows." Estlow laughed again, pulling her closer. He touched her throat with his tongue, kissed her bare shoulder. "And you," he said. "You bring the cops here. Now I will have to decide if it is better that you stay where you are or if I should move you again. Women. Nothing but trouble."

"I won't get into trouble again. I promise."

"You have promised before." He squeezed her arms.

"You're hurting me."

"Stay out of trouble this time." He kissed her again.

33

It was still dark when Diablo walked to Meigs Field, but soon it would be daybreak. The gates were closed and locked at night, but it was easy to go over the fence. There was no guard, but perhaps the police checked during the night. The blue plane with the black stripes was tied down where it had been when Riordan and Crosby were here. The key turned easily in the lock. Using a small flashlight, Diablo squatted under the control panel, and following a diagram, began to wire the detonator to the Pitot heat button, which prevented icing.

It was Thursday. Crosby should not come to the airplane today and even if he did, he would not fly until tomorrow, when the instructor came. They would fly out over the water, circling away from the shore. Would they need to push the button? It would be cold enough.

Crosby would die first, then Riordan, then Jamison and MacAlister, then Murphy. Murphy, the most predictable of all, going home in the middle of the day and always the same time at night, pulling into the garage, sitting there a few minutes with the garage door open. Murphy. Diablo could almost feel the weight of the gun that would kill him.

Diablo frowned. Maybe the bomb should be rigged to something else. No. The plane should explode in the sky. Then everything would fall into the water. Nobody would know what had happened. But the button would have to be pushed. It was not that important when Crosby died, only that he did not continue to live.

34

Ben was at the kitchen table reading the newspaper when Marti got home. Mike would be sleeping over while Ben worked his two-day shift. The house was quiet and with the light from the lamp not quite reaching the corners, the room had an aura of intimacy that Marti hadn't been aware of before. She sat in the rocking chair and closed her eyes.

"God, but I'm tired."

"You look worn out. How's it going?"

I feel like I've been wandering around getting nowhere for the past few days."

Ben put on the kettle. "Cocoa, tea, or warm milk?"

"How about some of that cider mix?"

"Sounds good."

It smelled good, too, a comforting cinnamon aroma that made her think of Momma. "I think Joanna wants to talk with you about something. Probably has to do with Chris. I told her it was a good idea."

"Chris and I went to her home game night before last," Ben said.

"It was a male thing, I suppose."

Ben chuckled. "I couldn't just stand by and let a nice boy like Chris let a little thing like testosterone get in the way of common sense."

"I figured it was something like that. Joanna said his mother keeps a supply of condoms in the medicine cabinet."

"Smart lady," Ben said. "Times are changing. From the looks of it, Joanna's one of the few young ladies on her team who wouldn't do just about anything to date him. That made it a little difficult for him to listen when she said no."

"Are they still a twosome?"

"For now. I think Chris is about to get a little competition . . . "

"For which I thank you."

"Any time." He brought the hassock over so Marti could put up her feet. Then he pulled his chair closer and put his mug of coffee on the small table by the rocker.

"Are you getting anywhere with this investigation?"

"Probably a lot further than I wanted to go."

She didn't mention getting shot at. She and Vik remembered a big, dark car, possibly a Lincoln. They still disagreed about the initials on the license plate.

"We took a trip to Eleventh and State and went through all of the reports," she said. "None of the physical evidence." She didn't think she would ever be able to look at or touch what Johnny had been wearing. "Just the photographs."

"You looked at the pictures?"

"Just one," she said.

Ben sighed, looked down at his hands, then at her. "You're stronger than I am. At the trial for the drunk driver who hit Carol, I couldn't look at anything at all, not even the street diagrams."

Marti didn't feel strong.

"Just before Carol died, I bought her a present, this pin I saw at the mall. I was saving it for Sunday, after church. She died Friday. When they leave like that . . . unexpected . . . When I decided to wait, there was no way to know I'd never get another chance."

Marti sat very still. She squeezed back the memory of the one gift that she didn't give Johnny until tears came to her eyes. Reaching out, Ben took her hands.

Marti spent Thursday morning at the precinct reviewing the notes she had taken on Johnny's death and mulling over what had happened since they decided to investigate. She called Ski and by nine o'clock had phone numbers for the uniforms first on the scene. James "Sully" Sullivan had retired, lived in Alabama, and refused to speak with her. Lefty Donovan had retired, lived in Kenosha, and also refused to speak. She had Lefty's address and intended to talk with him or get a door slammed in her face before the day was out.

Across from her, Vik sat hunched over a legal pad and his notebook. His wiry eyebrows were bunched in a frown. Marti's stomach growled. She looked down at a half-eaten burger and a half-filled cup of coffee, both cold. Breakfast—doughnuts and Mellow Yellow—had been been better.

"We need to start making connections," she said when Vik leaned back in his chair. "If there are any."

"Fayesta," Vik said. "Where in the hell is he?" Manuelito had returned Marti's call yesterday and called again this morning. He was convinced that Fayesta was dead. Marti had not been able to dissuade him. "Francisco Santos died somewhere on the north side." She checked the address. "That's not that far from where Manuelito lived. Manuelito and Fayesta were buddies, kept in touch."

"You think Fayesta could have known something or seen something?"

"I can't think of anything else that makes sense."

Vik's eyebrows furled.

"Skeptic," she said. "Maybe he'll call Manuelito again. There's not much we can do if he won't talk to us."

She could almost hear Johnny singing Chicomuno to a salsa beat. What had Chico seen or heard a year before their deaths? Why was Johnny meeting him that night? The Lopez bust had just gone down. That was the second bust that she knew of where Chico didn't get away in time but was released. Estlow was the dealer both times. Estlow, the Mexican connection. Chicomuno. The word danced in her mind.

Marti reached for the Tylenol. She shook out half a dozen Mylanta tabs, too.

"You're going to OD on that stuff," Vik said.

By one o'clock Marti and Vik were standing on one side of an old wood-framed screen door with a few holes poked in the mesh.

Lefty Donovan glowered at them from the other.

"We're all cops," Vik reminded him. After a moment, Lefty relented and allowed them to come in.

Everything in the living room except the table beside the recliner was covered with a thin layer of dust. Newspapers and magazines cluttered the floor. The mantle was crowded with framed photographs.

Marti sat on a couch with tattered antimacassars on the arms. Vik remained standing until she raised her eyebrows and glanced at a chair. Lefty looked from one of them to the other, still glowering. He looked old enough to have waited to retire until they wouldn't let him work a beat anymore. He wore bifocals and had thin strands of white hair combed across his head. Thin as he was, he had a pot gut and wore suspenders to hold up his pants.

"What is it you want? There's no need to come here discussing your husband's death, Miss. What's done is done."

"And what was done?" Marti asked.

"Nothing that wasn't proper procedure."

Ski hadn't given her any personal information about Lefty, but the room seemed so neglected and there were so many photographs that Marti guessed that Lefty had been married. At his age, being a widower seemed more likely than being divorced.

"He was my husband," she said. "Not just a cop. We have two children. I thought we would . . . get over it. That hasn't happened. It's there, all the time . . . the questions, not knowing."

Lefty stood up. "You think I didn't do my job?" he asked, waving his arm. "You think I lost those reports? They went missing after I'd typed them up and filed them. It was Holmes that changed his story when I asked him again. It was your husband's partner who changed what he said."

DaVon? Marti was stunned.

"What did he change, Sir?" Vik asked in such a quiet tone that Lefty calmed down.

"He said he was closer to the crime scene, that he didn't take as long getting there. He wasn't upset anymore. He was real calm the second time we talked. Ready to save his butt."

Vik and Marti were silent on the way back to Lincoln Prairie.

When they pulled into the parking lot at the precinct, Vik said, "What now?"

Marti shook her head. "It had to be Riordan who got to him. Riordan who took those reports. Riordan who had to save his butt."

Vik muttered a few curse words in Polish.

35

Frank Murphy spent the earliest hours of Thursday morning checking on his units. He stopped every hour or so to phone home and talk with Rozata. She sounded anxious, the way she always did if she was alone for too long, but Riordan was having him watched too closely. A day or two of good behavior should be enough to get rid of the watchdog.

It was almost daybreak when he got home. He pulled into the garage and just sat there. What in the hell had gone wrong? What had happened this time? How could his units keep screwing up? Where was the leak? He had watched the drug activity going on at that house, but when they went in, all they found was a hysterical woman and a bunch of crying, frightened kids. Who had it in for him? He'd be a laughing stock. This went beyond being set up. Whoever was doing this was having fun with him now. But not for long. Riordan would soon have his job.

As soon as Murphy opened the door, Rozata rushed to him. "Frankie, you are finally home. I'm so lonesome without you."

"You should be sleeping."

"No. I'm waiting for you." She pulled away. "You're not angry?"

Murphy could see her fear. He pulled her to him. "No. No. It's all right. You didn't do anything wrong. I love it when you wait up for me. I just want you to get enough sleep." Damn her old man Gianelli for beating his wife, for beating Rozata. They had been married for months. Would he have to reassure her forever?

"Is everything okay, Frank? Was the raid okay? Dan was worried—he called to make sure I was all right here by myself."

Murphy smiled as he stroked Rozata's hair. Crosby was as bad as Gianelli. Both of them retired and neither of them could keep his nose out of the job. But Crosby was a good friend to them both. The down payment on this house was his wedding present. Murphy looked at the clock. Three, maybe four hours and he'd have to get back to work.

"Let's go upstairs."

Rozata giggled.

When Frank awakened, Rozata was sleeping soundly. Propping his head in his palm, he looked down at her face. She was so young, so beautiful. One of Sergeant Gianelli's girls, promised to him since her junior year in high school. Married to him as soon as she graduated. After two wives, older and more experienced, Murphy found in Rozata everything he could want in a woman. He wanted to bury his face in her hair. He loved her hair, long and dark and soft, smelling of apricot shampoo, but he didn't want to waken her, not yet. Smiling, Frank went downstairs to fix Rozata's breakfast so that he could bring it to her in bed. To hell with the raid. To hell with Riordan. To hell with the job. He'd go and see Crosby later today. There were other things he could do. After all, Crosby was Rozata's godfather.

Riordan spent Thursday morning in his office, not even answering the telephone until after noon. Another "dead cert" raid had come up empty. All they found was a hysterical woman and two screaming babies and an apartment that had been cleaned out so fast there was only a TV and a sofa. And him, getting reamed out by the superintendent while everyone else at the table just managed to keep from laughing out loud. He couldn't trust any of those bastards, not one.

The aroma of the Colombian blend coffee he had to purchase himself for the office machine wafted in. Annoyed because his secretary wouldn't serve him, he let some of the coffee overflow onto the burner when he filled his cup, hoping the smell would annoy her. Murphy arrived exactly at one, as ordered. Riordan let him wait thirty minutes before inviting him in.

Then, Riordan busied himself with some papers and made a few phone calls, saving the most important for last.

"A place on East Fifty-seventh?" He paused.

"Right. Give me the address."

He repeated it.

"Sunday? Why Sunday? Hell of a day for a raid."

He laughed.

"Sure, you're right. Everyone knows the narcs are all in church."

He paused again. "Okay. Sunday morning it is."

Riordan hung up and looked at Murphy. "Newman will get the job done." He picked up a sheet of paper and recited what was written there without looking down.

"Monday. Arrived nine forty-seven, went home eleven fifty-three, returned two oh-nine, back home four thirty-two, back to work eleven after five . . ."

Riordan waited, but Murphy just studied the tips of his shoes. A few more pounds, Riordan thought, and he wouldn't be able to see his feet when he stood up. That little Italian wife of his must be cooking lots of pasta.

"You get a young bride, Frank, you've got to fit married life in during your off hours. No sneaking off two, three times a day to have a little fun."

"Whatever you say."

"No. We've been over this before. I don't want to hear that again. If you want a job and a wife, Frank, you have your ass here when you're supposed to. I'm not telling you that again. Understand?"

"Yes, Sir."

Five minutes after Murphy left, Riordan threw the marble pencil holder that Crosby had brought back from Ireland across the room. Murphy. That fat, lazy son of a bitch.

Murphy went to see Dan Crosby. As he followed Crosby down the oak-panelled hall, he peeked into the offices.

"What did you do, give everybody the day off?"

This was the first time he'd dropped in during the day.

"Seminar," Crosby said. "They're all boring as hell. I let the staff go and tell me what it was about."

Someday, when Murphy took early retirement, one of these offices would be his. Not that Crosby had offered him a job yet, but it was coming. Then Riordan could go to hell. *"Fungu,"* he thought. *"Fungu."* The thought pleased him. He'd give them all the finger when he said it.

"So, Frankie, how's tricks?" Crosby asked, bringing bottles of beer to the table by the window.

"Riordan's his usual pain in the ass. Nothing else going on."

"Come on, no big busts? I thought things had changed since I retired, that big boy Riordan and Riordan's Raiders were hot stuff."

Frank laughed. "Things were better when you were there, Dan. You knew what the hell you were doing. Riordan can't run that shop. It's too big for him. His operation is out of control."

"I know," Crosby agreed. "Joey's a detail man, a street cop. I never should have let them give him that kind of responsibility. Hell, I'm the one who recommended him, but you know, sometimes the man grows into the job."

Murphy took a long swallow of the cold beer. "You had the right idea, Dan." He swung the bottle in an expansive arc. "This is where it's at."

"You got that right."

"You been flying much lately, with the weather?"

"Couple times a week when it's not snowing. I keep her right here at Meigs." He winked. "Thanks to a friend who owes me a few. A few more lessons and I'll take you up and give you a tour of the lake. I could take you now, but this guy, what the hell, flying lessons are expensive and he's just a young kid, needs the cash."

As soon as Murphy finished his beer, Crosby brought him another. "Slow down, Dan. I've gotta drive home."

Watching as Crosby eased into the chair, Frank almost asked if his bursitis was acting up, but Crosby didn't like any mention of his health. By the time Murphy came to work here, Crosby would be ready to retire again and he could take over. If Crosby lasted that long. Damn. His color wasn't good, and Frank doubted that he ever used the exercise equipment.

Crosby belched, then raised his bottle of beer. "To the lovely Rozata."

"Yup. You should have married, Dan. It's great."

"The voice of experience speaking?"

"It just took a while to meet the right woman, but man, Rozata is really something."

Crosby looked at him. "What did I tell you? Get them young. Teach them. She's nothing like that blonde one you got mixed up with, is she? Or that little Irish spitfire. Gianelli kept Rozata in line."

Frank wanted to say that Gianelli beat Rozata bad enough to leave bruises, but he wasn't sure how Crosby felt about that. Dan never mentioned it, but when he talked about Gianelli, he never sounded disapproving. Did Crosby think he was beating Rozata?

Dan saw that his bottle was empty and brought another. "So, how's the job?"

"Life's a bitch . . . "

"That drug bust last night went okay?"

"No bust. No drugs. No nothing. Just a screaming woman and a bunch of crying kids."

"Frankie! After all the time you spent setting that one up? Timing, you know. It's the timing. They go in there for so many days, pack up shop, go deal some place else. You're off by a day and poof." He snapped his fingers. "They're gone."

"Yeah, well." Frank stifled his irritation. Crosby hadn't been on the street often enough to know what the hell he was talking about.

"Riordan on your ass?"

"You might say that. I'm going to transfer out of Narcotics, Dan, while I've still got a job. Things are really getting bad. If I didn't know better, I'd think someone had it in for me."

"Hey, Frankie, no. You can't do that. You gotta hang tough. This is just a streak of bad luck. Things will change. Soon. Look, let me talk to Joey."

"No," Frank said. "Please don't. I appreciate all you've done for me, but I think this is the right move. I've been a narc for a long time. Time for a change."

"Well, listen. Just sit on it for a while, okay. Just for a week or two. Things will get better, I promise. I was a cop, too, remember. Things like this happen. I know."

"You know, Dan, sometimes I think you want me to have this job more than I do."

"Being a cop, Frankie? There's nothing like it in the world. Nothing. Not one damned thing. Let's forget about this raid and this talk of quitting. What's new?"

"Nothing's new."

"Must be something, you've been keeping busy. I haven't seen too much of you lately."

"I ain't got a hell of a lot of anything going on. With Cantor dead . . . and Holmes. And now this. My guys are good, but the DEA liked working with Cantor. And Riordan's giving the good stuff to somebody else."

"Oh?"

"Yeah. Newman's got something big going down on East Fifty-seventh Sunday morning and I ain't in on it."

"I'll put in a good word for you when I see him. You're a good cop, Frank. A damned good cop. I tell your old man that whenever I get a chance to stop by. How's he doing?"

"Okay, I guess. With Rozata keeping me busy, I don't see enough of him either."

"Spend some time with him, Frankie. With your mother gone so young . . ."

"Yeah. I know, I will." Frank gulped down his beer. That bastard, the way he beat up on Ma. Let him rot.

"And Frankie, since you don't want Rozata to work . . ."

"Yeah, I know, Dan. She wants a kid, too. We'll name the first one after you, boy or girl."

Crosby watched as Murphy crossed the street and walked around the corner. Murphy couldn't leave Narcotics. Not when he was so close to getting Riordan out. He'd give Estlow this raid on East Fifty-seventh, lay off Murphy as long as he could, and talk to Joey.

Once Joey was here with him, Estlow could go to hell and Murphy would be just fine.

A few snowflakes drifted by. Crosby wondered how cold it would be tomorrow, if there would be any snow. He wanted clear weather all weekend. He wanted to fly. God, how he loved to fly. He went to the telephone.

"Yeah. You're okay at that house on East Fifty-seventh, but get your ass out of there before Sunday morning."

Hanging up, Crosby smiled. Poor Joey. He was in over his head. Joey was a cowboy when he worked under Crosby, couldn't follow orders. Soon everyone would know how incompetent he was. He never should have recommended Joey for his job. Cowboys didn't make good vice deputies. And they sure as hell didn't get to be superintendent.

36

When Vik and Marti got back to the precinct there was a printout waiting for them from the Department of Motor Vehicles. "Surprise, surprise," Vik said forty-five minutes later. Crosby drove a late model dark blue Lincoln, license plate number PG1074.

"Well," Marti said. "We now know two things about the man. He's a lousy shot and stupid."

"I would have expected more from a cop," Vik agreed. "Even if he is retired. How old is he? Maybe it's early senility."

"I'd guess he doesn't want me looking into Johhny's death. Question is, why? Maybe he was just trying to warn us off."

"Damned obscure way of doing it."

They went through their notes again.

"Nothing here to make Crosby stand out from the others," Marti said. "He wouldn't be my first choice for anything."

"Either we're getting close to something he doesn't want us to know or else we're sitting on something and don't know what we have."

"Let's lean on him," Marti said.

"Think so?"

"Why not? We could go around in circles on this one for months. At least we know we've got his attention. We know he does not want us investigating this case."

It was a little after eight P.M. when Marti and Vik took the elevator up to Crosby's suite. When they reached the fourth floor, a tall man in a bulky black overcoat was opening a door midway down the hall. Marti checked the suite numbers.

"I think that's him," Marti whispered. She rushed toward the man and caught the door before it could close. When he turned and pushed her she grabbed at his collar, pushed him inside and spun him around, taken aback by how old he looked.

"Crosby?" This wasn't the ruddy-faced Irishman she remembered. This man looked years beyond his mid-fifties. His skin was the color of putty and there were dark pouches under his eyes.

"Crosby," she said.

There was a wild look in his eyes. Fear, she realized as he clutched at his chest. Did he think he was about to be mugged? She let go of his coat.

"Go! Go!" he shouted.

She kept crowding him, keeping his back against the wall, not giving him enough room to move.

"Who are you? What do you want?"

She thought he would recognize her. "Marti MacAlister I'm a cop."

Crosby sagged against the wall. "Why are you here? Go away."

Marti let Vik step between them.

"You all right, Sir?" Vik asked.

Breathing hard and sweating profusely, Crosby nodded.

Vik closed the door. "Perhaps you need to sit down, Sir."

Crosby lurched away from the wall. They followed him down a short hallway. His footsteps were unsteady.

In Crosby's office, the sofa bed hadn't been folded away and on the desk, cereal floated in a bowl of milk. Crosby poured liquor into a paper cup and gulped it down, then poured a refill before sitting down at a table by the window.

"I don't know why you've come here," he said in a husky voice. "What do you want?"

"Why did you shoot at me?" Marti asked.

"Shoot you? You're crazy."

Marti took a step closer and he drew back. She stopped in disbelief. Scared sweat. She could smell his fear. Chicomuno, she thought. The raid where Fuentes said a cop took his gun. "What do you know about Chico Munoz?" she said.

"Huh? What?"

"And Hector Fuentes?"

"Get out!"

"How about Francisco Santos?"

Crosby went pale. He clutched at his chest. "Need something . . ."

"Fayesta LaVerne?" Marti said. Crosby reached for the liquor. His hand trembled so violently that the paper cup seemed to dance.

"Should we call an ambulance, Sir?" Vik asked. "You look like you might need medical attention."

"Out!" he said in a raspy whisper. "Get out!"

The door closed behind them. "I can't believe how much he's aged," Marti said.

"At least he's lived long enough to get old."

"You think he killed the kid? He reacted to every name I threw at him."

"We're getting too close to something he's mixed up in," Vik agreed. But with all of the damned covering up that was going on, when we figure out what it is, I don't think we're going to be able to prove any of it. Maybe Crosby will just drop dead."

"Crosby's a coward. If he killed Santos and Johnny found out somehow, or suspected . . . If Crosby had anything to do with Johnny's death, he didn't pull the trigger. If he was involved, I don't think we'll ever get to the trigger man. Maybe it was Munoz, another dead man who can't talk."

Marti didn't know what it would take for one cop to be involved with the death of another.

"Johnny would have trusted another cop," she said.

"I don't think Crosby would have had the guts to confront him."

"Maybe Crosby wasn't much of a cop, but if he shot the kid, Santos, why didn't he just call it in? He could have lied about what happened. They would have believed him."

"He was vice deputy, Marti. Even if it was ruled accidental he probably would have had to resign."

Johnny always said there were two kinds of cops: those who wanted to help people and those who liked the shape of the shield and the weight of the gun.

* * *

Crosby wiped his face with a paper napkin and downed another drink. His heart was still beating too fast. They could have killed him. Right there in the hall. Shot him and left him for dead. He had taken his hand off the gun in his pocket just long enough to open the door, and they could have killed him. He wasn't safe anywhere.

He picked up the phone. "Get her!" he yelled at the man who answered. "Get Marti MacAlister! Now! Or that house on East Fifty-seventh is the last thing you ever get from me."

37

Diablo watched from the roof across the street from Leotha Jamison's building. Eight apartments, four up, four down. Three couples, three singles, and two old ladies. Diablo had been watching off and on for several weeks. All of the occupants who worked were out by seven-thirty in the morning. It was Friday, and last Friday none of them had returned right after work. Last Friday morning at ten o'clock someone had come for the little old lady who lived in the apartment beneath Jamison's. Diablo wanted to know why.

At nine o'clock Diablo parked an old pickup truck in the alley behind the building and went inside, using a duplicate of a key stolen two weeks before when the other old lady's purse was snatched. The landlord was too cheap to replace this lock, or thought it was unnecessary.

Inside, Diablo began on the first floor, whistling and making noise, unfolding the step ladder, opening the smoke detectors to remove the batteries. Soon, the old lady with blue rinse in her hair, and thick eyeglasses, and hands crippled up like claws, opened her door. Stupid woman. Anyone could be in the hall. Diablo explained about replacing the used batteries with new ones.

"That's one of the things I like about living here. The maintenance. My daughter wanted me to move in with her, or at least into senior housing nearby, but she lives in Peoria, and she has four children, and none of them have any manners and I know I'd have to baby-sit. Besides, I can't stand her husband." She lowered her voice from something that wasn't quite a scream to something that was too loud for a whisper. "He's borrowed money from me, you know. I think he gambles. Anyway, my youngest, Beatrice, she and her husband have a condo on Lake Shore Drive and no children. Every weekend I apartment sit for them. There's a doorman and everything. He's a doctor. She used to be a nurse but now she just does volunteer work."

When the old woman came up for air, Diablo asked to use the bathroom. The old woman's television was going full blast and she sat on a hassock with her face close to the screen. The bathroom was right by the bedroom, the woman's purse and coat laid out on the bed. Inside the purse was a key ring full of keys, and in a small pocket another with just two keys. Spares, in case the others were lost? Diablo gambled that they were keys to the front door and apartment and took them.

When the old lady's daughter came to pick her up, Diablo was in the basement, shutting off the water main that was hooked up to the sprinkler system.

"Mother, would you please hurry up? I have to be at a luncheon by noon."

"Of course dear, just let me lock this door. Always better to have a deadbolt, you know."

"Did you bring all of your medication this time? If I have to run out again to get a prescription refilled . . . "

"Now don't you worry about a thing, dear. I've got everything that I need."

Before leaving, Diablo used one of the keys to go into the old lady's apartment and poke through her things. Real silver, good jewelry. Out of habit, Diablo pocketed a few pieces. "Keep an emergency stash of small things easily sold. You don't know when hard times will come," Diablo's cellmate had warned.

Diablo checked the closets and decided that the fires would start there. Two fires, both away from the door. The pyromaniacs in jail liked to describe elaborate setups, but those who set fires because they were paid to do it always said, keep it simple and make sure you have a way out and enough time to get out. Diablo wanted a fire that would spread quickly, too, so that Jamison would not be able to escape. Smiling, Diablo got the closets set up. Tonight all that would be necessary was the accelerant and the fuse.

38

Marti woke up with a headache Friday morning. By 9 A.M. she had taken three Tylenols and two Contacs and still had a headache. As she reached into her desk for more medication, Vik said, "Maybe that over-the-counter stuff isn't strong enough. Maybe you need a prescription."

Before she could respond, Slim and Cowboy came in.

Slim danced over to Marti's desk, did a complete spin, and gave her a dimpled smile. "Guess what you're not going to read about in the newspaper today."

"You caught the old guy who was exposing himself in the nursing home but he's the mayor's uncle so you're keeping it quiet," Marti said. It was pointless to complain about his cologne anymore.

"The little lady's closer than she knows," Cowboy drawled, pushing back his five-gallon hat.

"It's Jessenovik's uncle?" Marti asked.

"It's too many antihistamines," Vik said. "You're getting wired."

"The Dyspeptic Duo is grumpy again," Slim said. "This department just set a record for folks not killing each other around here and you two are acting like we got a serial killer out there."

"We responded to a call of indecent exposure," Cowboy said, "and found a recently defeated alderman, buck naked and dead drunk, with an unclothed companion in the mayor's office."

Vik knew who it was. "The man was an imbecile when he was in office. No reason to change now. The *News-Times* ought to put it on the front page."

Marti reached for the Tylenol.

"Uh, uh," Vik said.

She unscrewed the cap. Maybe she did need a prescription. "Hey Vik, check your notes on Fayesta. Remember all those prescriptions? What was the doctor's name? Maybe he's had him call in a refill."

A few minutes later, Vik said, "Doctors. Eight to be exact."

Half an hour and six phone calls later, they located Fayesta in a hospital in Chicago. Marti called Leotha, who said she could stay with Fayesta until they got there.

"Fayesta's been admitted to two hospitals since we last saw him," Vik said on the way out. "Resourceful, isn't he?"

Marti's headache intensified when they got stalled in the express lane on the Kennedy Expressway, waiting while an accident was cleared.

Marti yawned.

"You're not getting much sleep, are you?" Vik said.

"Cat naps," Marti admitted.

"Do your kids know what you're working on?"

"No, I haven't told them."

"It might be a good idea if you did."

"Think so? You talk with Mildred about the job?"

"Sure. I'd tell her something like that."

"Does she worry?"

"I don't think so. Not much anyway. Mildred's not much of a worrier."

Joanna was. Theo, too. Were they worried about her now? She wasn't working a case, as far as they knew, but she was away from home a lot. "What about your kids?"

"They didn't get a rundown of my day, but we never went out of our way to keep anything from them. Steve's like his mother, never worries about anything. Grades, job, nothing. Jasna, she was the quiet one, like Theo."

Jasna was the artist. Pottery, painting, sculpting.

"Mildred had to talk to Jasna a lot. Her imagination would go wild. You wouldn't believe what the kid could do with a traffic bust. Too much TV."

Is that what Theo did, imagine things? She and Johnny had never told him anything. If he knew more since they moved here, it was inadvertent.

Fayesta was in a two-bed room, hooked up to an IV. The other bed was unoccupied. Leotha sat facing the door.

Fayesta didn't look away from the TV when they came in. "What you want? How you find me?"

He was wearing a wig, but the covers went straight to his chest; no breasts today.

"I need to know what made you run," Marti said. "Why are you hiding?"

"Been having trouble with my ulcer."

"That's not what Manuelito said."

Fayesta thought about that. "Can you get me to St. Louis if I tell you?" he asked.

"Maybe. Depends on what you got, and if it's a good enough reason. What's in St. Louis?"

"I got people there. My sister's there and my aunt."

"Why aren't you there now?"

Fayesta closed his eyes. "Would you want me around?"

"What's happened to change that?"

"Nothing. But as long as I keep to myself and away from their friends, they won't throw me out."

"Okay. What you got?"

"I was in the alley the night the kid got killed, in a doorway, taking a leak. They got these Dumpsters. He couldn't see me."

"Who?"

"The guy that done it."

"You saw him?"

"Heard the shot, crouched down behind the Dumpster quick. Guy was all in black, hat pulled down on his face, wearing gloves. He walked under a light. I saw enough to know who he was. A cop. His picture'd been in the paper, but I'd seen him besides that, cruisin' them alleys. We knew to watch out for him. Time was he'd beat the hell out of one of us. It was the big one, Crosby."

"Why didn't you tell?"

Fayesta gave her a derisive look. "I told your husband. Couple days before he died. Look what happened to him. What you think would happen to me?"

Marti stared at him.

"I got the hell away from there," Fayesta said. "Didn't nobody come lookin' for me, so I figured he hadn't had time to tell. Then you come, and then, right after, he come. Crosby. Why you think I ran? Sergeant Jamison here, she say you just want to know how your husband died and don't know nothin' about that man, but he know about me. Ain't no way I can leave here now 'lessen I go to St. Louis. Might not even be safe there."

Leotha left the room and got an off-duty friend to come over, supposedly for Fayesta's protection, but also so that Fayesta couldn't disappear again.

When they went to the parking lot across from the hospital, Leotha said, "Let's go up to the fifth level. That's where Cantor went over."

The wind was cold and sharp at the top, the sky a faded but clear blue. There was a helicopter on the hospital roof. Marti could see the Sears Tower. They went to the ledge and looked over.

"His partner was one level below," Leotha said. "I finally got him to tell me what he knows. The dealer moved up the time of the exchange. Cantor and his partner had already gotten the buy money from the DEA agent, so what the hell. Of course Murphy cautioned his men not to do anything like that, but it amounted to the same thing as permission for all the attention anyone pays to what Murphy says. Word is that Murphy's on his way out. Point is, Cantor had the drugs on him when he died and those guys don't like to leave their shit behind. Makes it look like they were there to get Cantor. It was business as usual until he went over this ledge. They must have known he was a cop."

"Maybe he asked the wrong person about Johnny."

Leotha pulled out a pack of cigarettes. "*That* we don't know for sure. Cantor hadn't said a word to his partner about that."

"Well, we do know that Crosby killed that kid. Johnny knew, too. I'm going back to see Rivas."

* * *

This time Marti called first. They agreed to meet Leotha after their meeting with Rivas.

"You're sure this is what you want to do?" Vik said. "We could go to the lieutenant or the state's attorney."

"No. Chicago has to be able to police its own. I worked for this department for ten years. And Johnny . . . we'd still be Chicago cops if he . . . " A cop. Crosby. She felt nauseous.

Rivas came from behind his desk and extended his hand to each of them.

"MacAlister, Jessenovik. Good to see you again."

Marti told Rivas everything she knew. When she was finished, Rivas looked at her. "MacAlister, Johnny talked with me about a week before he died."

"What? Why didn't you tell me?"

Rivas turned his hands palms up. Why didn't Johnny tell her? What did he tell Rivas? Whatever it was, it was more than he ever said to her. Why didn't she know any of this? She wasn't just his wife, she was a cop, too.

Rivas took a manila folder from his desk and handed it to Marti. "This is the order that your husband's deck of cards was in."

They hadn't been able to crack Johnny's code. There was something she knew that they didn't. Marti started to decode the card order, saying nothing and hoping her face was inscrutable.

"You let them say he committed suicide," she said.

"None of us knows what happened that night. Based on the evidence . . . officially, it was accidental."

"That meant nothing to his children. Who knew he had come to you?"

"Nobody."

"But someone could have suspected something. Are you still investigating his death?"

Rivas smiled. "You've had much more success than we have."

Marti read the code. She thought of the rearranged cards that she had held so often lately.

"If you had given this to me sooner . . . "

Rivas nodded.

"Johnny says Crosby killed Santos, names Fayesta as an eyewitness, says Munoz saw Crosby take the gun."

"Is there anything else?"

"Just a name, Diablo, and the symbol for danger."

Rivas made two phone calls, the first to send someone over to get a statement from Fayesta, the second to the state's attorney's office requesting a warrant for Crosby's arrest.

When they left his office, Vik said, "Typical cop. He didn't tell us a damned thing."

39

Riordan sat at his desk, gouging holes in the wood with the letter opener. Crosby. The leak was Crosby. Riordan didn't know who Murphy was talking to until Murphy told him. He never would have suspected Dan.

Murphy, that fat son of a bitch, had turned in his gun and his shield. Now he was talking to Rivas.

"I killed them," Murphy said, dry-eyed and calm. "I trusted him. I talked too much. I killed them."

"Killed who?" Riordan asked.

"DaVon Holmes. I told Crosby about that raid. And Julian Cantor. I told Crosby about him, too, when Cantor asked me some questions about Johnny MacAlister."

MacAlister. Why did his name keep coming up? What had Marti MacAlister talked about with Rivas today? According to his source, Rivas was having a warrant issued for Crosby's arrest.

Now he was waiting: for Rivas to call, or the superintendent. When Crosby went down, he would go, too. Riordan felt the wood give and pressed the blade deeper. So what if the Lopez raid paid for Crosby's retirement? Riordan still would have made vice deputy without Crosby. He didn't need Crosby to get where he was. This wasn't Bridgeport and Crosby wasn't big brother anymore. He didn't owe Crosby anything.

At this desk, in this office, Crosby had failed. Riordan ran the offense, Riordan took on the bullies, Riordan saved Crosby's ass. Crosby, always the coward, had hidden behind this desk while Riordan worked the street. And now Crosby, that bastard, was sabotaging his operation. Why? So that Riordan couldn't do something Crosby hadn't done first? A bunch of dogs, his uncle had warned. They will snap at your heels like a bunch of hungry dogs.

Riordan went to the window. Crosby liked to think he'd got him into this job. Maybe, if Riordan pushed the right buttons, Crosby could help him stay here. The man wasn't well. Maybe, if he knew what was happening, he'd just go away. Skip the country, have a heart attack, eat his gun. Without Crosby, they couldn't prove a damned thing.

Crosby went to the window and gripped the sill with both hands. No hit man out there. None that he could see. The windows didn't open.

The raid on East 57th went down on the wrong day. Estlow had been arrested. He'd seen it on the twelve o'clock news. Joey must have set Murphy up, but he was the one who would get burned.

Crosby dialed Estlow's number. "It's okay. Everything is okay. We can still deal. I didn't do it. It wasn't me . . . It . . . it . . . it was Frank Murphy. Lieutenant Frank Murphy, the narc who told me. They were setting him up. They don't know it's me."

There was a loud click.

"No!" He dialed again, got a busy signal. "No!" He stared at the receiver, then slammed it down.

A voice? He spun around. Who? Where? The television. He rushed over and turned it off. The phone rang. Estlow's men! He could deal!

"Dan, it's me, Joey. You'd better get in here right away. They're trying to get a warrant on you."

Crosby dabbed at his forehead. Arrogant bastard, talking to him like he was some kind of criminal.

"Sure, Joey. What's this about?"

"It's about some kid who got shot four years ago, Francisco Santos. You know anything about that? And Murphy is babbling something about Cantor and Holmes, too. You better get your ass in here and tell me what you know. Maybe it's not too late to cut some kind of deal."

Bastard. It was Joey's ass on the line, not his. If it wasn't for him Joey wouldn't have that job, and now Joey wanted to use him again. Well, Joey didn't know it yet, but he was through running interference for him. Let Joey get himself out of this.

"Sure Joey, whatever you say. We'll talk. This is all just a mistake. Just some damned mistake. A hundred years ago, Joey, damned near every cop in this city was Irish. Being a cop was good then, honorable. Now we got affirmative action. The whole damned department's gone to hell since we started letting everyone in."

"Right, Dan. Just come in, will you? I just talked with the superintendent and bought you some time. I don't want to see you coming in here in cuffs, Dan, and being locked up in a cell."

"Thanks, Joey. Just give me an hour. Traffic. I'll be there."

Joey owed him. Joey owed him big time. He'd go away for a few days, let Joey worry about him, let Joey think about how much he owed him. He could explain whatever he needed to. He just needed a few days to think.

Crosby went to the window again. He could feel, even hear his own heart beat. He looked out. No cars parked out front. Nobody waiting. Would Estlow's hitman let him know if he was there, dare him to come out? Maybe he should go out the back way. No, he'd still have to get to his car. Traffic. He could lose them.

Crosby gripped his gun. What if they were waiting for him to come out? He went to the door and opened it wide enough to look into the hall. Nobody. He cradled the gun in his arm with his finger on the trigger and kept his back against the wall as he walked to the elevator. When the doors opened he crouched, pointing the gun. Empty. He didn't conceal the gun until he was inside and the doors closed.

Johnny MacAlister. This was all MacAlister's fault. The man made a fool of him, finding crack cocaine where there wasn't supposed to be any, finding shit that wasn't even supposed to be in this part of the country. This was his city, not MacAlister's. It wasn't New York. It wasn't L.A. Johnny MacAlister should never have been allowed to become a cop. He was the worst kind, trying to bring another cop down, calling him a killer because he shot that Santos kid in self-defense, trying to turn him in to IA. MacAlister. A bad cop, rotten to the core. And now his wife wouldn't leave him alone.

40

When Marti parked near the restaurant where Leotha was waiting, she felt a sudden depression set in. She had gone into this without knowing how things would turn out, but whatever the reason, this outcome was disappointing. Maybe it was just that she could find no satisfaction in having another cop involved.

Marti let Vik tell Leotha about Crosby.

"What?" Leotha said. "The man's got an airplane. Somebody's warned him by now. He's probably left town."

"An airplane?"

"Yes. Just one of those little ones with a propeller, but it flies."

"Rivas must know that."

"Sure, MacAlister. And Crosby still has friends in the department. Riordan, for one. Don't be surprised if he manages to get away."

"Where does he keep it?" Marti asked.

"Meigs Field."

By the time they reached the turnoff to Meigs Field, they could see Crosby's car parked in the fenced lot.

"What did I tell you," Leotha said. "You see anyone here from the department?"

Crosby rushed to his Cherokee Six, untied it, climbed on the wing and jumped inside.

What now? What to do? Door. Latch the door. Seat belt. Electrical equipment off. Fuel pump on. Headset on. Yes! He could fly! He could fly this baby all by himself.

Prime the engine. Right mag to second position. The propeller was spinning! Second mag. A loud roar! Yes! Throttle forward. He turned on the electrical switch. He was moving! He called the tower on 121.3 and was cleared for take-off on runway 36, so he taxied into position and pushed in the throttle for take-off. He could fly! He could fly!

His headset muffled the sound of the engine. He could hear other pilots talking to the tower. Looking down, he saw the three of them on the airstrip. He laughed and turned the nose east, toward the lake. He loved flying over the water. He'd go to Racine or Milwaukee, then give Joey a call, let Joey take care of all of this for him. He had always taken care of Joey. It was Joey's turn now.

Crosby leaned back. He eased his grip on the yoke. Clouds overhead, lake below, everyone far away. The plane began to fight a head wind. Turbulence. He looked to the right, saw a large white cloud extending maybe ten to twenty miles across the sky. A snow squall. What to do? No ice. No ice on the wings or he'd go down.

By the time Marti reached the fence, Crosby's airplane was taking off. Marti ran until she saw a young woman standing by a white plane about the same size as Crosby's.

"Can you take us up there? Can you follow that plane? Do you have enough gas?" She flashed her badge.

"Sure, lady," the freckled-faced young woman said.

"Can you fly this? Are you licensed?"

"Yes, ma'am. This baby's mine."

Vik and Leotha caught up.

"Got room for my friends?"

"Sure. Better hurry. Up on the wing and in the door."

The six-seater was cramped inside. Marti sat up front beside the pilot.

"Put on your headsets, everybody. Cuts out a lot of the noise and we can talk to each other."

"Can anyone else hear us?" Marti asked.

"I'm the only one who can communicate with the tower. Here we go."

As Marti watched, Crosby gained altitude. "Hurry up."

"Three-six-five-six Whiskey to tower."

They were cleared for departure and assigned a runway. Marti wanted to close her eyes as the plane gained speed and left the ground. She couldn't believe she was going up in the air in something this small. When Vik didn't say anything, she turned to him. His lips were compressed, and he looked pale.

"Motion sickness, Jessenovik?"

"No. Temporary insanity."

Leotha didn't look too happy either.

As the pilot adjusted her headset, Marti said, "What's your name?"

"Katie Franklin."

"How high are we going, Katie?"

"We're climbing at five hundred feet a minute. We'll level off at about seventeen hundred to two thousand feet. A mile is five thousand seven hundred thirteen feet. That's as high as we can go until we're out of Chicago Class A airspace."

To the west, Marti could see land. To the east, ice formed along the shoreline, with blue water farther out. The lake. She hated flying over water.

"Can you see him?"

"He's pretty far ahead, but I've got him."

There was a huge cloud ahead of them, extending hundreds of feet above them and spreading across the sky for miles. "What's that?"

"Snow squall. We're going to stay clear of it. He'd better head for land."

Marti looked down. For a moment she thought of Julian Cantor. Wind buffetted the plane. This was crazy. What if they went down?

Crosby's plane shook. Everything was white. He couldn't see the ground. He stared at the control panel. Buttons, levers, switches. Which one? Think, don't panic. Think. No ice. He could go back to Meigs if he had to. If the carburetor iced he'd be in big trouble. Prevent icing. Pull out carburetor heat. Keep the air-speed indicator working. Prevent . . . the Pitot heat button, which one was it? There. That one. He reached for it.

The plane seemed to jump as Marti heard the bang. She gripped the sides of the seat as the plane shook.

"It's okay," the pilot said. "We're under control. I'm going back."

"My God," Marti said, "Crosby's plane!" A fireball plummeted to the lake. "Crosby's plane. It's gone."

As Marti, Vik, and Leotha watched, the Chicago Coast Guard Search and Rescue Team patrolled the lake in slow, wide circles. Accompanied by the Coast Guard Rotocraft, they were looking for debris from Crosby's plane, and possibly a survivor.

Riordan stood next to them. "I can't believe this. I just can't believe it. He knew he couldn't fly. He knew it."

Nobody answered.

"I can't believe Danny went down like this," Riordan said. "His instructor showed up right after I got here. I can't imagine what could have made him decide to go up by himself."

41

Out of habit, Riordan almost drove by Crosby's place after he left Meigs Field. Poor Danny. But what a way to go, in the proverbial blaze of glory. Riordan checked his rearview mirror. The little silver Geo that had been tailing him was still trailing behind. He stopped at a fast food place and took his tray to a seat by the window, feeling exposed but making sure his tail could see him. After a few bites he got up and went toward the bathroom, ducking out the side door and keeping close to the building. The Geo was parked half a block away. He could see someone sitting inside.

Riordan stopped at a gas station, then checked his rearview mirror. When he was four blocks from home the Geo pulled into the turn lane and made a left. He had noticed someone standing in doorways several times this week. Who was having him watched? Rivas? One of Crosby's old cronies? The superintendent? What did they expect to observe?

Traffic was light in the north side area where he lived. He wished he could go to the condo near the lake—more security there. Damned divorce. Never again. He thought of the schoolteacher he'd met the other night. Maybe. He was a sucker for blondes.

Instead of going to the garage, Riordan parked three blocks from his street. A blast of wind hit him as he got out. Damn, but it was cold. Winter had come early this year and was probably going to stay late. For once Riordan wished for a hat.

He unholstered his weapon, concealing it in his pocket, and walked a circuitous route, two blocks, then one. He checked out the apartment buildings across the street first, approaching from the alley, checking doorways and rear stairwells. Two blocks from home, he crossed the street and approached his building the same way. He circled around to the front and checked. He saw nothing. Nobody standing in a doorway. If he could just catch the bastard, he'd know who had ordered the survelliance. He decided to leave his car where it was. The street was dark but the car had an alarm.

As he let himself into the apartment, Riordan felt the adrenaline ebb. He threw his coat over the back of a chair and sat on the sofa without turning on the lights. The furnace kicked on. The refrigerator stopped humming. The back stairs creaked.

Riordan got up and eased his way to the back door, listening. Silence. Nothing. He waited until his shoulders ached from standing in one position. The stairs creaked again. He opened the apartment door with his weapon drawn.

"Freeze."

Downstairs, the door opened. As Riordan ran down, cold air hit him in the face. Outside, someone sprinted away.

"Stop! Police!"

The person kept running. As he followed, Riordan tried to gauge height and weight, but just saw shadow, dark clothing. Garbage cans clanged as the person ahead of him threw them in his path. Whoever it was kept getting farther ahead. When he reached the end of the alley, the street was empty.

Riordan leaned against a building for a moment, gulping in the damp air. With his weapon still drawn, he went to the spot where he had last seen the person turn, checking each door along the way. Nobody. He was only a block from where his car was parked.

Diablo watched as Riordan got into his car. Did he know what it was like to be set up, to be hunted down like an animal, to be afraid? Was he sitting there looking out, afraid of who was looking in? How had he felt, knowing he was being watched, knowing he was being followed? Diablo would have liked to play the game a little longer, but the longer the game went on, the greater the risk of getting caught.

Diablo squeezed the trigger. Unless someone knew what a gunshot with a silencer sounded like, they would hear only shattering glass.

42

Incredible," Leotha said, as they sat around her kitchen table eating pizza. "One minute Crosby's up in the air, next minute he's gone."

"Right," Marti said. "And now he can't tell us a thing."

"There's still too much we don't know," Leotha said. "Too many details there's no way to fill in."

Vik popped open a Pepsi. "We told Rivas one hell of a lot more than he's told us."

Marti thought of the code in Johnny's cards.

"If Munoz knew Crosby had taken that kid's gun for almost a year, I wonder what he needed from Johnny to tell him about it when he did?"

"At least we have a motive," Vik said.

"Be nice to have a perp, too."

The description she had of Chico Munoz wasn't that of a cop killer. Crosby's motive was more than sufficient for murder, but she didn't think Crosby would have had the guts to stand toe to toe with Johnny and pull the trigger. How had somebody gotten that close? Maybe she was wrong and it was Crosby. He was a cop. Who else would Johnny have trusted? And Diablo. Danger. What did that mean?

Leotha's beeper went off and she went to the phone. "What? You've got to be kidding. Who? . . . Son of a bitch."

"Well, I'll be damned," Leotha said when she hung up. "Riordan's dead. Someone shot him while he was sitting in his car."

"Riordan?" Marti said.

"And Crosby," Vik said. "In the same day."

Marti ran her fingers through her hair. "Riordan. Why? Suppose this goes back to when the gun was stolen and the kid got shot."

Vik got out his notebook. "Run a raid by us, Leotha. Assuming Johnny set it up, how would it go down?"

Leotha gave a quick explanation.

"So," Marti said. "Riordan would have come in afterward. We know Crosby was there. And Johnny set it up. Munoz would know that."

But who would care? Not the victim's family. Santos's mother had OD'd. There was just the grandmother and his siblings.

"Santos was the oldest kid?" Marti asked.

Leotha nodded.

"No other relatives here?"

"None that we know of."

Hector Fuentes. They did know his relatives.

"Are you still being followed, Leotha?"

"Not for the past couple of days."

"Any reason why Fuentes's brother or sister would be out to get you?"

"Me? Hell, it's been three, four years since I arrested her. The charge was reduced to a misdemeanor. She walked after a few months in county jail."

"Could be revenge," Vik said. "But odd choices. Crosby makes sense, but the others? Holmes and Cantor didn't have anything to do with that bust."

"Then let's just leave them out of it for now," Marti said. "Concentrate on those who did. Crosby took the gun, used it, Hector took the fall. Plenty of motive."

"Crosby wasn't exactly an easy target," Leotha said. "He hardly ever left his office."

"But Johnny was. And if Munoz told what he knew . . . "

"To who?"

"I'm guessing Fuentes's sister or brother," Marti said. "The sister is a user, has been busted for using drugs. Her brother was at that raid. They must have known the same people."

"We'll have to see how much of it checks out," Vik said.

"Timing," Marti said. "We need Juanita's arrest record."

Leotha reached for the phone.

In the apartment below, Diablo went to the closets and put the accelerant and fuses in place. Jamison would die tonight, too. Too bad there wasn't some way of telling them why they were dying, but if they knew, Diablo would get caught. There were three cops upstairs. Let them all die. Hector was as good as dead.

There had been three of them at the cemetery that night. Johnny MacAlister was in the car with Chico, and Diablo was hiding in the trees. When Chico made MacAlister angry and MacAlister grabbed him by the shoulders and shook him, it was easy to hit MacAlister on the back of the head. Chico had grabbed his bag of strychnine and cocaine and run before Diablo put MacAlister's hand around his own gun and pulled the trigger.

Diablo did not know about bombs and fires then. Killing Mac-Alister seemed like nothing compared to what all of them had done to Hector. MacAlister was a much easier target than the others before Diablo went to jail and learned new ways to kill.

And Chico, that rat, setting them up, bragging that he could not be arrested, knowing all that time that MacAlister was setting up the raids and Crosby had taken Hector's gun—and saying nothing until Diablo forced him to tell what it was that he knew. Diablo wanted to tell Estlow who had killed MacAlister but could not. Estlow believed in his own luck. He never noticed how somebody else made it happen. Maybe now that Crosby was dead, Estlow's luck would begin to run out.

Diablo pulled out the box of wooden matches. Now all of them would be dead except Murphy. Diablo had all night to take care of him.

Leotha wedged the telephone receiver between her neck and shoulder and made a few quick notes. When she hung up, she said, "Doesn't sound like much to me, but then again, folks kill each other for nothing every day."

"What have you got?" Marti asked.

"Juanita Fuentes was in jail during her brother's trial."

"Because you busted her?"

"Yes. But she's a junkie. Do you think she's smart enough to do all of this?"

"Her or the brother. If her drug of choice is cocaine, you know how aggressive that makes them." Marti was finally beginning to see a pattern. "It's a good place to start." She sniffed. "Do you smell something burning?"

Leotha sniffed. "No."

"I don't either," Vik said, "but Marti can detect Obsession for Men at two hundred feet."

Leotha went to the door and touched the doorknob. She opened the door a crack and slammed it shut.

"Smoke. I can't tell where it's coming from. I've got to get Jaws out of here."

While Leotha went to cover the bird cage and put it out on the patio, Marti went to the phone. "Line's dead."

Vik went into the bathroom.

"Eight apartments?" Marti asked.

"Four up, four down, no vacancies," Leotha confirmed. "Fire doors at each end of the hall. You and Vik take the back. Two old ladies downstairs in the front apartments. They know me."

"I need another towel," Vik called.

Leotha directed him. "I've only got two flashlights. When you get downstairs, just twist the doorknob. The back door opens out."

Vik passed out wet towels. "Let's go."

They crawled out of the apartment and closed the door. "Smoke's worse," Leotha said.

Vik panned the hall with the flashlight. "Can't identify the source. I'll take that side. Stay with me." Crawling fast and staying near the wall, they began yelling "Fire!" They came to a door and pounded on it.

One man came out. "Get down," Marti ordered, handing him her towel. "Anyone else up here?" The smoke made her cough. She wrapped her wool scarf around her mouth.

"I don't know."

They met Vik at the fire door.

"It's not hot," he said. "Let's go."

The stairwell was filled with smoke. Marti could taste it.

"You okay?" Vik asked as she began coughing again.

"Yeah," she gasped. She could hear the fire crackling. Smoke swirled around her. "It's coming up. Downstairs fire door must be open."

"Getting hot," Vik said. "Hurry up."

The lower she went, the hotter it got. "We're going into it. Let's go back up."

"It's coming up!" Vik yelled. "No time to get to the roof. We're half a landing from the back door."

"No," the man said. "I'll burn to death."

Marti grabbed his arm. "Move!"

Vik stayed ahead of them. When he reached the first floor hallway, he peered around the corner with the flashlight. "Fire's confined to the apartment beneath Leotha's. When we open this door the air is going to pull the fire toward us. Move fast. Smoke's bad."

"Wait," Marti told the man.

When Vik yelled "Now," she screamed, "Go!" The man froze. Marti grabbed a handful of hair and yanked. "Go now or die!" Crouching, they made it outside.

Marti gulped in the fresh air and vomited. Her chest hurt so bad she couldn't run. Vik put his arm around her waist and led her away from the building. Gasping, Marti collapsed on a pile of snow.

"Damned good thing you smelled smoke," Vik said.

In the distance, she heard sirens.

Marti didn't think she could spend another five minutes in the ambulance. Vik had gone to check on Leotha. Marti pulled off the oxygen mask and took a few tentative breaths. Her lungs didn't hurt much.

"I've got to get out of here," she said. "The arsonist is probably out there and thinks I'm still inside."

"Look, ma'am," the paramedic said, "I understand, but you ate a lot of smoke this evening."

Paramedics were always so damned calm.

"You just stay on that oxygen. Someone else will take care of whoever did it."

"There is no one else!" Yelling set off another spasm in her chest. When the coughing and gagging subsided, she put the oxygen mask back on. The odor of smoke made her nauseous. Her hair, her clothes. She must have absorbed it into her skin. Marti felt as tired as she'd ever felt in her life. She lay back on the pillow.

Vik came to the ambulance door a few minutes later.

Marti lifted the mask. "How's Leotha?"

"They transported her and the old lady she brought out. Smoke inhalation. No burns. The bird's even okay. By some miracle this is still a code green—no serious injuries or crispy critters."

"Thank God they haven't found any bodies."

"Yet," Vik said. Soot streaked his face and his eyes were red. "Look what I've got." He handed in two sets of fireman's gear. "Guess what we're going to be?"

"Hey, wait a minute," the paramedic said. "This officer needs medical attention."

"You feeling okay?" Vik asked.

Marti took a deep breath of oxygen, took off the mask to cough more, and nodded.

"Good."

The boots were too big. "Can't you get anything smaller? These are like boats," Marti said.

Vik took his off. "Try these."

They fit her feet with her shoes on. When they were ready, Vik said, "Guess what?"

He held up a camera. "You're a fire department photographer now. Go work the crowd. I won't be too far away."

Marti grabbed the camera and equipment. "How do I look?"

"Like you just spent half an hour in hell."

"Maybe I need more soot. If either of the Fuenteses did this and they're out there, they'll recognize me."

Vik studied her face. "You can see where the mask was." He rubbed her cheeks. "Looks okay."

"They've got another photographer out there, don't they? I don't really have to take pictures?"

"Let's just find them," Vik said.

The fire had stayed in the apartments at the front of the building, but more units had been called in. Marti counted four engines, two trucks, and a snorkel squad. She was able to identify several battalion chiefs and a deputy district chief. The flames had spread upward and burst through the roof.

Marti checked the camera and changed from a wide angle to a zoom lens. Amid engines and hoses and the firefighters' shouts, a sense of order prevailed. Marti moved to the edge of the firelines, toward the crowd. She estimated seventy-five to eighty-five people. A fire buff, accustomed to seeing a fire department photographer at the scene, smiled and waved for the camera.

Uniforms patrolled the perimeters, warning off children who tried to duck under the barriers. Marti kept a careful eye on the crowd. She could not name the person she was looking for, but she would know who it was when she saw them. Despite the change in Marti's appearance, that person might recognize her, too.

"Hey, over here!" a teenager called. "Take my picture."

Must not be a gang member, Marti thought. She aimed and pressed the shutter. She moved slowly, unable to be unobtrusive, amazed by the rapt expressions on the faces of some of the onlookers. How could anyone enjoy watching a fire? Too bad they were outside. A crawl through would change their minds. She coughed and heard a wheezy rattling in her chest. It would take days to cough up the smoke.

A face in profile caught Marti's attention. The woman turned. Their eyes met. Juanita Fuentes recognized Marti and began to push her way through the crowd.

"Stop her!" Marti shouted. "She started the fire."

Police, the crowd, and Marti converged. People were shouting and pushing as Marti tried to shoulder her way through. The crowd shifted into a circle. Marti shoved her way through to the center. Several men were on the ground, arms flailing. Uniforms pulled the men away. Juanita Fuentes got to her knees. Blood streamed from her nose. One eye was swollen. Her coat was torn. She sat back on her haunches and looked up at Marti.

"You bitch," Juanita said. "You're supposed to be inside."

43

Ben drove in from Lincoln Prairie to take Vik and Marti home. It would be hours before the streets were cleared and they could get their car. Marti went to the back of the van. There was enough room to lie down but not to get comfortable. Up front, Vik told Ben what had happened. When Ben shook her awake, Marti sat up, inhaling the odor of smoke.

"You're home. A lot of lights are on. It looks like everyone's up and waiting."

Joanna and Theo. Maybe she should go over to Ben's and clean up first. No. There was already too much that they didn't know. Too many secrets. This was part of her job. It might happen again.

Ben helped her out and put his arm about her waist as they walked to the door.

"My God," Sharon said. "Are you okay?"

Theo and Joanna rushed over. Theo threw his arms around her, hugging her tightly.

Joanna stood back and looked her up and down. "Ma! What happened? Vik said you were at a fire, not in one."

Marti went into the kitchen. "How about a cup of tea?"

"Rosehips?" Joanna asked.

Marti remembered the caffeinated tea leaves she had added to it. "No, something else. Sassafras." She wanted to sleep.

Theo sat on the hassock near Marti's feet and put his head on her lap. "Are you okay, ma?"

"I'm fine. Someone started a fire in an apartment building while Vik and I were inside." She described exactly what had happened.

"Weren't you afraid?" Theo asked.

Marti stroked his hair. "I was afraid. But there isn't time to think about that when something like this happens. We had to get out. We're trained to get out. We know how to exit a burning building. We've practiced—with real fire and real smoke."

Theo sat up. "Was it real smoky?"

She nodded.

"And dark?"

"Uh huh."

"Could you see the fire?"

"No. It was still confined to one apartment."

"And you rescued somebody?"

"Sure did."

"Will your picture be in the paper?"

"I don't know."

He grinned. "That is so cool. Wait 'til I tell the guys."

Joanna brought her tea. "This is awesome, ma. Just awesome."

"There's something else," Marti said, amazed by the way they were accepting this. "It's about your dad. Vik and I have been trying to find out what happened. We don't know everything yet, but we think we've got the person who killed him."

Nobody spoke. Joanna stood there holding the cup and Theo sat stock still. After what seemed like a long time, Theo whispered, "I knew it. I knew he wouldn't leave us on purpose."

44

With few interruptions, Marti slept almost round the clock from the time she got home early Saturday morning until Vik called her late Sunday morning.

"Where are you, Jessenovik? You're not at work?"

"Don't worry about that. You stay home. There's not much to catch up on. We got the reports back on the skeletal remains."

"You still haven't had your fill of reports? I thought all that time you put in the annex at Eleventh and State would cure you."

"These really are old bones, Marti. They think it's some French settler who will remain nameless forever. The lieutenant's preparing a news release. Wait until you get a look at the forensics."

Marti smiled. There was no cure for the man. When she got up, the kids had gone to church, but Sharon, who usually went with them, was sitting at the kitchen table.

"You okay?" Marti asked.

"Umm humm."

"You don't sound okay."

"She had the baby."

"Oh." Marti pulled up a chair.

"She called," Sharon said, "to tell me Frank Junior weighed seven pounds, nine ounces, and his daddy was right there when he was born."

A little boy. Marti thought of Theo when he was just a few hours old. She remembered Johnny's face the first time he saw his son and how pleased she was that Theo looked just like his father.

"When Lisa was born, Frank was studying for midterms. My girlfriend had to take me to the hospital."

Marti wasn't convinced that Sharon didn't still have feelings for Frank. Love wasn't rational. She avoided saying anything negative about him, even though she disliked him. "You were both young then."

"No, that's not it," Sharon said. "Frank never wanted Lisa. I went off the pill anyway. He was furious when I got pregnant. Of course, he didn't want me either, not permanently. He just wanted a meal ticket, a free ride while he got his master's. I thought once the baby was here things would change . . . and maybe if it had been a boy, if Lisa had been Frank Junior, things would have been different."

Sharon jumped up and poured two cups of coffee. When she returned to the table, Marti said, "Johnny wanted me to have another baby."

"Right before . . . "

Marti nodded. "I think . . . " She took a deep breath. "I think he had some . . . premonition. He was so insistent. Get pregnant now, Marti. Now. That wasn't like him. I thought it was . . . he was almost forty. You know how men get sometimes. He thought I was off the birth control. I didn't tell him I was going to wait."

Tears gathered in her eyes and trickled down her face. "I thought there was time . . . I thought . . . we could wait . . . I didn't know he was going to die." If she had gotten pregnant, their baby would be almost two and a half. Johnny wanted to name it for her father if it was a boy.

When Marti arrived at Rachel's house Sunday night, the elderly aunt let her in. Rachel was in the kitchen at the stove.

"Marti! It's so good to see you!" She frowned. "What's wrong?"

"I'm fine."

"You're not fine. Come. Sit down."

Marti looked at the bare tree branches for a while, remembering the squirrel whose life was saved by the snow. There hadn't been enough of a snow cushion for Julian. And all because of a frightened coward of a man who was brave enough to kill a child.

"What is it? What have you found out?"

Marti told her.

"Why are you sad? You caught her. You caught the one who did it."

"It was stupid and senseless, all of it."

"And not what? Not brave? It didn't take bravery to go to the cemetery, to go up on the roof? Not smart? Hindsight is smart. And it didn't make sense? When you're a cop the world does not make sense."

Marti didn't have any answer.

"I have asked myself all of this, Marti. Why, why, over and over again. Know what? I don't know why. And I'm not going to know why. Now at least I know what happened. I know Julian was doing his job. I know he was trying to find out what happened to a friend. He was doing mitzvah. Johnny was doing a mitzvah. That's good Marti, that's good. Some of us just die."

Marti took both of Rachel's hands in hers and squeezed. "You do a mitzvah, too."

Before heading back to Lincoln Prairie, Marti returned to Eleventh and State for what she hoped would be the last time. Rivas was waiting. She felt a sense of dread as she went into his office. Outside, the sky was dark. Another storm was moving in.

Rivas leaned back in his chair and rested his chin on the tips of his fingers. He looked at her for a moment. "Estlow and Juanita Fuentes are talking," he said. "Angelo and Diablo. They're doing their best to tell enough on each other to cut a deal that will keep them off of death row, none of which I can tell you about. At least not at this time. I think you know all you need to about Juanita. We do have a case."

"Her brother," Marti said. She understood the guilt that would force Juanita Fuentes to blame everyone but herself, but still felt angry. If the woman hadn't helped her brother become a criminal in the first place . . . maybe that was feeding her guilt.

"They think they're so smart," Rivas said. "That cocaine tells them they can do anything, and get away with it. 'The cocaine made me do it.' The state's attorney laughed in Juanita's lawyer's face when he suggested insanity. I'll tell you as much as I can about what happened that night."

Marti sat dry-eyed while Rivas described what had happened to Johnny in the cemetery. "I cannot undo what's been done, but I think there should be some private ceremony for you and your children. They should know that their dad really was a hero."

He opened his desk drawer and took out an envelope. "We'll turn the rest of Johnny's personal effects over to you as soon as we can. I thought maybe you'd like to have these now."

Her hand shook as she took out the "Lucky Looney" key ring that Joanna had made out of a coin brought back from their Toronto vacation, and a bracelet that Theo had made for Johnny at Cub Scouts. An Indian symbol for father was tooled into the narrow strip of worn leather. Things Johnny must have kept with him that he didn't think anyone would pay much attention to. Johnny never wore any kind of scent or clothing he thought would cause someone to remember him while he was undercover, but he had let Marti choose the small dragon tattooed on his shoulder. She didn't know that he also wore the bracelet and carried the key ring.

It was late when Marti got home. She gathered everyone, including Ben and Mike, in the family room. She sat with Theo on one side and Joanna on the other and told them what had happened to Johnny. "There were trees and it was damp. It had rained. You know how he felt about places like that. A lot of what we do depends on instinct. Sometimes, our life depends on instinct. If your dad felt uneasy that night, he might have thought it was because of where he was at, not who he was meeting."

She explained the investigations Johnny was involved with when he died. "Your dad needed to be a narc."

"Because of his sister," Joanna said.

"And because he was so much younger than she was, and there was nothing he could do to try and help her."

Marti took the bracelet and the key ring out of her pocket. "He kept us with him," she said. "All the time." She hugged Theo and gave him the bracelet, hugged Joanna and gave her the key ring.

"He had these when he died."

Marti reached into her purse and took out her wallet. She showed them the snapshots taken right after their birth. "I have to go to work tomorrow, and I know it's not always safe. But I keep you all in my heart, all the time."

She looked at Sharon and Lisa, then Mike and Ben, and smiled.